P9-DMK-565

STREET
LEVEL

STREET LEVEL

BOB TRULUCK

THOMAS DUNNE BOOKS
ST. MARTIN'S MINOTAUR
NEW YORK

www.minotaurbooks.com

Library of Congress Cataloging-in-Publication Data

Truluck, Bob (Robert)
    Street level / Bob Truluck.—1st ed.
        p. cm.
    "Thomas Dunne Books."
    ISBN 0-312-26626-X
    1. Private investigators—Florida—Orlando—Fiction. 2. Orlando (Fla.)—Fiction. I. Title.

PS3570.R817 S77 2000
813'.6—dc21

00-040236

10 9 8 7 6 5 4 3

STREET
LEVEL

1

If there was a significance, I wasn't getting it. I turned the sketch 180. It still looked like an eyeball with wings.

"You had it right the first time."

I looked over at the guy I was sharing the booth with and grunted. "What's it supposed to be?"

I got a shrug that said he hadn't spent a lot of time thinking about it. "A flyin' eyeball."

I was thinking this was not the person whose name was on the check lying between us on the Formica. The one for five grand. If he was, and that's what he thought I was asking, he would have grabbed his check and been on his way.

"Yeah, I got that part. What's it mean?"

"It's just a tattoo, so far as I know."

I put the drawing down and looked at the guy. He was boring me.

We were in a round corner booth at a chili joint called Angel's on the south end of Orange Blossom Trail, and the guy was sitting closer than I would have preferred. The waitress drifted by; he ordered food, I didn't.

A couple of county cops showed and started in with the waitresses, the ladies laughing, acting bawdy for the heat. One of the cops was talking to a girl, maybe our waitress, I wasn't sure, the other one checking out the room. When his gaze slid past, I gave him a decent upstanding-citizen smile, as decent and upstanding as I can do sitting in a grease trap at two o'clock in the afternoon with a fat guy wearing a plaid hat and a shiny suit.

With all the guy was giving to go on, I felt his best bet was a psychic with a bloodhound. We were wasting each other's time, and I wasn't hungry, so I tried to put the conversation out of its misery. "Where do you find a hat like that?"

He looked up like he could see the narrow brim snapped over his eyes and grinned. "St. Paul," telling me he was proud of it by the way he laid it out.

"St. Paul?" He nodded me on. "What'd you say your name was? John?"

I knew that wasn't what he had said his name was, but no surname had been offered. I was trying to prompt him. I didn't expect it would work, and it didn't.

"Don."

I pushed the check back in his direction, threw the drawing on top of it, said, "Tell you what, Don. You go on back up to St. Paul and tell the man who writes the checks that he'll have to do better than this."

Don's eyebrows did a jig. So did his Adam's apple. "This is not sufficient to meet your needs, Mr. Sloan?" putting four syllables to *sufficient*, pointing at the check.

I shook my head. "The five's fine. But tell your guy that I don't have the resources or the inclination to find some nameless girl who might be in the Orlando area. Somewhere. We don't know what she looks like, but she's maybe pregnant and she's got a flying eyeball tattoo." I gave him a sincere grin, said, "She might stand out back home in St. Paul, Don, but down here she's just

2

another white girl with ink on her ass. Tell him the money's nice, but I need a little more to go on. And I'm sure your man's got his reasons for sending you to check me out instead of coming himself, but I'm gonna need to hear a little more of the story, too. And I'd prefer to hear it from him. He wants to arrange something, you let me know."

Don was grinning, looking smarter than I thought he could. "This man will want to know something."

"What's that, Don?"

"He will want to know if you are good enough to justify these demands."

"And what'll you say?"

"I will say you have decent stats."

"And what'll he say?"

"He will say if you are so good, how come you did two years in a federal penitentiary and still do not have a valid investigator's license."

He caught me cold. I'm sure it showed.

Don was kind. "What will I say, Mr. Sloan?"

I caught up with real time, said, "Tell him I've got a letter from the Feds saying it was all just a big misunderstanding."

Don nodded, he liked that. "I will tell him this."

Don's chicken-something came, and I left him with it. I was thinking I'd wasted the afternoon on something I'd never hear from again.

Three days later the mailman dropped the same check at my place. No note. No nothing. Just an envelope with the check for five big fish.

2

Someone with a more complex philosophy and a less developed cynicism would have secreted the check away, I suppose. Put it in a safe-deposit box or some ingeniously camouflaged hidey-hole, waiting for that phone call. I deposited it in my checking account.

Don's reluctance to put a name with his benefactor or share with me who I should thank or blame for the referral had worked as planned. My curiosity had been aroused.

By the time the check had officially cleared, I knew the man with the proud handwriting was a guy named Isaac Pike, money so old they may have had some of the original stuff laying around. And since he was somebody who probably paid more to the IRS every year than a guy like me would make in a lifetime, I overcame any noble urges that may have been lurking about, said fuck it, and went to Costa Rica on the five. Chump change to a guy like him. Flew first class and had too many drinks.

The next morning something caught up with me. Maybe a hangover, maybe my conscience. I dug out the number Don had written on the corner of a napkin and called. When I had him on the line, I told him where a guy from Florida might be found when he was on vacation, said, 'bye, and hung up. If we were all on the same page here, I'd be seeing Pike down here in banana land. If I was wrong, then I'd just have to suffer through a few days in paradise.

Four days later, I was lounging in a beach chair behind a place called Selvan's Cabanas down at Playa Negra on the Caribbean side. I was watching the waves punch the coral rocks that boned up the beach, wiggling my feet into the silty mush that passes for sand here, wondering why the brown buzzard a few yards away was eating a cracked coconut. Wondering if all his brown brothers shunned him when he got back to the roost every night with coconut breath. Before that, I was wondering if all women really are sisters. Major cerebration on weighty subjects.

The shadow startled me, but I knew who it would belong to.

"Aren't you Duncan Sloan?"

"Not right now. Right now I'm just a guy on vacation."

"Mind if I pull up some sand, Mr. Sloan?"

"Who says I'm Sloan?"

"Mind if I pull up some sand, Mr. Sloan," like he hadn't heard me.

"Pull away, Mr. Pike. You're paying for it."

We sat that way for a bit, the ocean slapping hell out of the rocks, the sun toying with the mountain tops behind us. A decent breeze was bringing in a clean smell from the east, pushing the saccharine stench of the heliotropes back into the jungle.

"I'm glad to see that you were expecting me." Silence. "I wasn't exactly sure if I was supposed to come or not. I like your choice of meeting places, Mr. Sloan."

"Yeah. We'll have to do this more often."

"I hope not." Silence. "I've got a few questions before we get to it. Some background stuff. You mind?"

"Not much." I was thinking maybe I should be asking my questions first.

6

"What happened? Seven years ago?"

I was still looking out to the ocean; I still hadn't turned to look at Ike Pike. "You ever been married?" I knew the answer.

"No."

"Then you couldn't know what it's like to be riding in the ambulance with your boss who also just happens to be your ex-father-in-law, him a nice purplish blue. Second heart attack in as many years. He's sucking on the mask like it's life itself, looking at you like there was something you could be doing about it."

I looked over at Pike. He was a decent-looking man with pale gray eyes set in etched features. Not rugged but close. Young looking for the forty-four I knew he was. He was wearing a tan print silk shirt with natural-colored linen trousers. Expensive-looking loafers; no socks. Dressed like a rich guy. Too fucking tense, like a rich guy.

I don't like rich guys, and I didn't want to like this one. I had been doing a pretty good job so far. But when he smiled, he gave up something from inside, something almost vulnerable, like that version of sadness only the chronically lonely can know. "And I know what I should have been thinking."

"But, instead, you were thinking . . . ?"

"I was thinking: God, please don't let this motherfucker die and leave me to work for my bitch ex-wife."

Pike laughed quietly. "So an interesting independent opportunity came along and you reacted?" He had heard the story before. I guess he just wanted to watch my face while I told it.

"You follow right along, Mr. Pike. But in all honesty, boredom was probably as a big a factor as any. Yeah, I reacted. Against all instincts and advice. I took on a job gathering information for some guys who are in a very exclusive club. When the information was used as a lever in some extortion, things blew up. My clients went back to Jersey and I went to jail. It wasn't the smartest thing I've ever done." I gave him a shrug. "I paid for it."

7

"You won on appeal, though."

"Yeah. Well, it's not like I was vestal. The guy I dug dirt on killed himself. I was cut loose because they couldn't put balls to the conspiracy thing second time around."

"Were you conspiring?"

"No." I had put it out there too quick.

"No, but . . . ?"

The guy was a listener, a rare and refreshing quality in the wealthy. Hell, a rare and refreshing quality for anyone.

"The term *conspiracy* can cover a lot of issues, and I don't feel that refusal to identify a client is necessarily conspiracy. And maybe I watched too much TV as a kid, but I don't see any future in rolling over on wise guys."

That seemed to be good enough for him, since he was nodding like he believed me. "You did what? Two years?"

"Close."

"Country club?"

"That's what they call it. Personally, I found it a bit more confining." That got me another sad smile. "My turn?"

He said yes and steepled his fingers against his lips.

"Who gave me to you?"

"One of my security people. Jay Feingle."

Feingle had been with Costa Security, my ex-pa-in-law's outfit for a while when I was there. I didn't care much for him. I had thought him a little too clean for his own good then, but that was back before I had my ethics adjusted by the Feds.

"How long has Jay been with you?"

"Four years now. You're wondering why he's not doing this, right?"

I was wondering exactly that and said so.

Pike gave me a happier version of the smile, eyebrows up, "He says you're better than he is." He let it float, then, "Are you?"

"Depends. Jay's good at what Jay's good at."

"He says you're the best there is off the beaten path."

"I'm not sure that's a compliment."

"I think it was meant to be."

I doubted it.

We sat some more, watching skimmers not much bigger than hummingbirds work the evening buffet. I couldn't come up with a more civil way to go, so I said, "The girl. Don's description doesn't sound like someone you'd be interested in."

That got an honest chuckle and a peek at the edge of a secret. "No. No, that's not my type at all."

I would have asked what his type was, but I had pretty well figured that part already. "So what'd she take?"

"You follow right along yourself, Mr. Sloan. Actually she didn't take it. But she supposedly ended up with it." He held up with that.

Good listeners can be as goddamned exasperating as they are refreshing. "You think I'm gonna need to know what it is?"

The places I've been in, the spots I've been put on, the jams I've weaseled my way out of, I get to thinking that it's almost impossible to get a fastball by me. But Ike Pike did.

And when he did, I began to get it. One word, and the pieces began to fall into place.

He said, "Semen."

3

Elena's was, and may still be, an open cafe about a quarter mile up the dusty road from Selvan's. You can get a fried fish, intact head bristling with sinister teeth, covered in an indigenous tomato sauce. Or you could get a cured pork chop, chicken, or something resembling beef, all fried, all swimming in the same sauce, but mercifully without the heads. Elena herself is an ebony pixie, bright green eyes and businesswoman's smile. If she happens to be on-site, she may bring her Red Stripe and a delightful island accent to your table and make you feel nearly local. If you have business, she will leave you to it.

Pike had said he had a folder for me, and I had suggested we trade the gusty beach air and humidity for the dust and heat at Elena's. He agreed, and we had shaken hands and gone over to first names. He then left me and my buzzard friend to our weighty thoughts of shunnings and sisters.

A cool shower and an hour later, I found Pike at a quiet table at Elena's. Don was with him, plaid hat and what had to be a new outfit: one of those matching shirt and shorts beach things— magenta with big white hibiscus silhouettes scattered about on it.

He had traded the big black brogans for faux leather sandals but had kept the thin black socks. Don didn't really need the required tourist ID card. He was wearing it.

With them was a compact man, quick dark eyes and an expression that said he was not going to be my friend. He wore a sleeveless tank over a barely adequate pair of shiny athletic shorts, the ones with the rounded slit at the sides, and about two hundred dollars' worth of sneakers glowed new and white on his feet. He had one of those flat-link gold chains just big enough for the circumference on his neck and what could have been about two thousand dollars' worth of wristwatch. I knew who he would be.

As I made the table, Isaac Pike and Don stood, the small man did not.

"Nice outfit, Don. Good color on you." I put out a hand and Don matched it twice over with his own.

"Thank you, Mr. Sloan." I think Don may have blushed a little under the plaid hat. "Very nice to see you again."

I got my hand back and offered it to Pike. He took it and I said, "Ike."

The dark man bristled at my reference to his lover as Ike. I knew Pike went by Isaac, but had found the rhyme irresistible, and it didn't seem to affront Pike.

"Duncan. This is Steve Glass," the standard hesitation, "my partner."

I tightened the lower part of my face into something resembling a smile; Glass didn't. He clipped, "Charmed," without looking at me or taking the hand I had been passing around.

I couldn't help it. I said, "Likewise, I'm sure."

Glass put the mean dark eyes on me like I was an unpleasantry he had found on the sole of his shoe. "Really?"

I bumped back. "No, but I'll endure."

That seemed to be enough; he coolly conceded, "Have a seat."

"Thanks, Steve," got me a warning not to push it from the baby doe eyes. No, Steve Glass and I weren't going to be buddies.

Elena came over, kissed me on top of the head, and asked what I would be drinking this evening. I told her I'd like to see the wine list. She brought me a sweaty Red Stripe.

There was an accordion file on the table, and I pointed, said, "For me?"

Pike pulled out the sad smile. "Yes. I hope it's adequate. Jay threw it together pretty quickly. I hope it's in an acceptable format."

I said, "I'm sure it'll be fine," with no idea if it would be or not. I wasn't sure I'd know acceptable format if I was looking at it.

I rolled the woven band off with a banjo twang and dumped the contents on the table. On top was another check. Same as the first five grand. I was starting to feel like a high-dollar whore.

I pushed the check across to Pike and said, "I don't need this yet."

That amused Pike. "Duncan, do you really have that big of an aversion to my money, or is this some self-imposed antimaterialistic thing you've taken on?"

I said, "Yeah," looking to confuse the matter a little.

It didn't work. Pike said, "That's what I thought."

We traded smiles.

Next was a courtesy memo from Jay Feingle; looking forward to hearing from you, looking forward to working with you again stuff, and the usual battery of cell, pager, office, voice mail, et cetera numbers. I licked a thumb and moved it off the pile.

A blown-up mug shot–style photo of a Latino with plenty of *negro* in his tree was now on deck. I sort of moved my head in Pike's direction, putting a question mark on him with my brow.

Pike: "His name is Manuel Quesada. He worked at the fertility clinic. He's the one who—"

I helped him. "Nabbed the tadpoles?"

Glass rolled his eyes, turned forty-five degrees, and put a leg on a knee.

Pike said, "Yes." There was more but he bit it off.

I studied the tough face in the grainy photo, licked the thumb again, and slid it over. I saw why Pike had balked: a newspaper clipping stapled to an obit run, both dealing with Manny Quesada, dead man.

Seems Manny had floated up on the banks of the Minnehaha Creek in St. Paul despite several ounces of lead he was holding in the back of his head. That partially answered the question of why we were creeping around like cold war spooks. I had a feeling there was more to it than that.

"Anybody got a clue?" I knew the answer.

Pike looked at Don, who was poking at one of the new plastic sandals. Don looked up, said, "Oh." His head wobbled around like he was going to shake an answer out of the plaid hat. He pursed his lips and pushed them around some, I guess to warm them up. "No, Mr. Sloan. No takers on that one. The police seem to think it was drugs."

"And no one up there wondered if it was related to the fact that the dead guy was trying to extort money out of the Pike family?"

Glass stood, said, "I've had enough. Isaac, you want to waste your time and money on this comedic keyhole peeper, that's you, but I refuse to participate."

Pike put a hand on Glass's arm and said, gently, "Steve, come on now. Jay told us what to expect. Didn't he?"

"Jay said, and I quote, 'Sloan is a little irreverent.' He said nothing about being a disrespectful wise-ass." Glass shrugged Pike's hand off and said, "I'm going back to the room." He left.

After a small punctuation of silence, Pike said, "Sorry, Duncan. This is tough on Steve. He's been pretty I-told-you-so since this thing started exploding."

"I take it he's not real keen on the idea of motherhood."

Pike smiled one of his amused smiles. "No. He can't see why I would want to disrupt our lives this way."

I didn't say it, but I had been belaboring the same question. Why would a rich gay guy decide he needed to be a parent? For the life of me, I couldn't figure what engine would drive such a desire. One that went against all convention and society's view of parenthood. Maybe I was a little more bigoted than I would care to admit. And I couldn't help but wonder why I thought that part of it was any of my fucking business.

But mostly, I wondered who had iced Manny Q, and where it fit in with all of this. And if someone had this much stake in keeping Ike Pike from being a parent, then the girl with the flying eyeball inked on her ass was surely living on borrowed tomorrows.

The next lick of the thumb got me one I'd seen before. The tattoo sketch. Old news. Under that was one I had been waiting for—the letter.

It looked as if it had been put together by someone who had been watching TV when he should have been in school. It was a crude collage of different-size cutouts from magazines. It read: WE THE ONES GOT YOUR CUM. GOT IT IN THE OVEN. WILL CONTACT WHEN IT GITS DONE. DONOT CALL POLICE. IF YOU DO WE WILL HAVE ABORSHUN. GIT AHUNDED THOSAN DOLARS REDDY (the amount appeared to have been pasted over several times). REMEMBER DONOT CALL POLICE. SINED ANGELS EYE.

Not exactly master's thesis stuff but beefy on succinctness. About what I would expect from the guy in the mug shot. I guess that made the tattoo on the girl's ass some sort of proprietary stamp. Maybe gang shit.

Now I was looking at an artist's sketch. The girl. It appeared to be an enhancement of an attached photo that was too small and of too poor a quality to do much good.

I was expecting something different and I guess it showed. Pike said, "She looks about twelve, doesn't she?"

I agreed. She looks like what Carville was talking about when he mentioned what you get when you drag a hundred-dollar bill through a trailer park: thin, dirty blonde hair that would always look like it could use some shampoo; thin, lipless grin; little pointy elf ears; and eyes that seemed to be appraising me even from the picture. She looked like she'd probably been trading pussy for what she needed since she was about nine and a half. Eyes way more demimondaine than angel.

Last was a chronology of events, how the girl was tied to Quesada, what Jay had plowed up on them and their lifestyle, that kind of stuff. Her name was maybe Crystal Gail Johnston, born in Orlando, Florida, 1981, and their lifestyle was titty bars, rock cocaine, and convictions for B and E. Manny had been on work release and the state had gotten him the job at the clinic. The boy was a heads-up opportunist if nothing else. As it turned out, maybe too much so for his own good.

Most of the stuff, Jay had gotten from a contact in the police department in St. Paul. Pretty good investigative work with a nice kicker. A hot credit card that Manny Q had been videoed signing had worked its way south. Last register: a flophouse called the Hio Motel, Orlando, Florida.

That was it. Not as much as I would have liked, but a hell of a lot more than what Don had brought to Orlando last week. I grabbed the pile and bounced it on its end to align it and slipped it back in the brown folder.

I drained the now warm Red Stripe, and sat back looking at Pike.

"Well?" he said.

I pressed my own thin trailer park lips together and puffed my cheeks. I turned the captive air loose with a drawn-out *pooh* sound. I said, "There's some stuff I've gotta know," then held up.

Not-as-dumb-as-he-looked Don pushed himself up with big hard hands and said, "Mr. Isaac, I think I should go check on Mr. Steve. Do I come back for you?"

"No, Don. I'll get Duncan to drop me by when we finish up," then to me, "That work?"

I nodded, and Don excused himself and rumbled off in nylon socks and plastic sandals as quietly as a Mack truck with a loose recap.

"Good man," I said to his back.

"The best," said Pike.

"How long's he been with you?"

"Third generation for both families."

"Damn," was all I could think of.

Elena brought two more Stripes and left them with a sultry wink. Pike and I sat, picking at the labels on our beers. A foraging ant stung me on the ankle and I stamped my foot and rubbed the spot.

"How did Don get the gun down here?" I had noticed the bulge even under the loose festive shirt.

"He picked it up locally. From the man who runs the place where you are staying, I believe."

I nodded. I'd been staying at Selvan's for years and knew he was a dabbler in arms and parrots. "Would he cap someone? If need be?"

"If I asked, I guess he might."

"Would you?"

There was a tad of offense, the first I had gotten from Pike. It went away and he said, "If you mean Quesada, the answer is no. Why? I'd find the hundred thousand to get the child. Maybe more if need be."

"Who else does he listen to?"

It took Pike a few difficult seconds to say, "My father."

I could feel my head nodding. "How does he feel about all

this? Your father, I mean?" I figured Don pretty much felt like he was told to feel. With three generations, you get lots of training.

"He's not thrilled."

"Adamantly?"

"We are both being too generous. No, Duncan, my father doesn't feel that queers have earned the right to parenthood. And my father says what he thinks. He can afford to."

The next one was tougher. "Does he object adamantly enough to have Quesada capped?"

When Pike looked up several beats later, his eyes had a slight glisten to them. "I'd hate to say."

"That sorta sounds like a yes."

Pike shrugged.

"Your mother?"

"Dead since I was six."

"Siblings?"

"One sister." He was thinking.

I shrugged an answer out of him. "She's very sanctimonious. Evangelical. TV stuff."

"Enough said."

Again we sat.

"Is there anyone else worth a mention?"

Pike shook his head, making trails in the condensation on his beer with a thumbnail. "You don't think we can find the girl without rolling a lot of stones over?"

It was my turn to shake my head. "Not a chance. Honestly, Ike, I'm gonna be damned lucky to find her before Manny's shooter does. You realize this?"

He said he did.

"I'll be looking for her, but in the meanwhile, I'll be dancing around with whoever it is. I may not know it, but I will." I gave him some time, then said, "What do we do with young Crystal, should I locate her?"

"I haven't gotten that far yet."

"Then you need to. I would suggest giving her a big chunk of money, in escrow, then we stash her until we find our mystery player."

"What if he never shows up?"

"He will." We were assuming women don't do the two-to-the-back-of-the-head thing, I guess. "He'll be right behind me. Looking over my shoulder. He'll eventually get around to busting a cap or two in my direction, I expect."

I'd not heard Ike Pike use any of the profanity that seems to roll off my own tongue so eloquently, but he finally did. He said, nearly in a whisper, "This is getting out of fucking hand."

I thought I'd cheer him up. "It's *been* out of hand, Ike. We just didn't know it."

"I think I did. I just didn't want to admit it."

"You know, you could drop all this, let the cops do their thing, go adopt a kid. It's not unheard of nowadays." I had a friend in a similar situation in New York. He had adopted recently, and there seemed to be a rash of it going around. I told him about it.

Pike was shaking his head. "My father. He has extremely long arms to go along with the deep pockets."

"You've tried?" I noticed I had gone from asking pertinent questions to being nosy.

"Yes. Several times. It hasn't helped that Steve is not excited, but my father has really been the one pulling the pin. Each and every time."

I got the sneaking around. We were hiding from Daddy. I let it go. "There are several other countries on the globe that don't begin with USA. You tried Mexico?" My friend had; it worked for him.

Pike smiled me the sad one. "Graft is the political lubricant in Mexico, and the farther south one goes, the worse it gets. No, my father is quite adept at getting what he wants. Regardless of where it is."

"You want this kid, don't you, Ike?"

The shine was back in his eyes. "You couldn't begin to know. And this one, I feel like I have a God-given right to." He looked over at me for verification and I fumbled.

Then Ike Pike went somewhere I wasn't sure I wanted to go, but the guy needed somebody to hear him out. I was handy.

"My entire life, that love that I'm not supposed to be able to give, that parental connection, has been held over my head like a club. Yanked back when I dared to be less than the perfect son. Used to beat me over the head. Threatened to be disowned, disinherited, cast out.

"When I came out, my father didn't speak to me for over two years, Duncan. When Steve and I moved in together, another year. My sister, the devout hypocrite, still barely acknowledges my existence." It was getting lumpy and he stopped.

I was stumbling around, trying to figure what I was supposed to say here, came up with, "How's this going to help?" I meant his relationship with his family but he took it another way.

Pike looked up from the spot on the table where his eyes had gotten stuck. "I want to love this kid. I want to give this kid a love that doesn't require qualification. I don't care what she or he ever does or doesn't do, what it becomes or doesn't become, or how disappointing or embarrassing the child may be to me or my family." He stopped, pulling himself back inside the shell. He looked almost angry now. "I want to do this better than my father did. I want to love this child just for being mine, no matter what sort of six-headed monster it may turn out to be. Do you understand that, Duncan?"

I said I did, and I wanted to but, honestly, I didn't think anyone but someone just like Isaac Pike could ever understand what he felt.

4

Pike and I picked at dinner, and I dropped him at the ritz joint he was camping at about nine-thirty, quarter of ten. Back at my place, I packed up, turned the lights out, and sat in the dark smoking cigarettes and sipping *guaro*, the local excuse for rum. I was trying to get all the plays and all the players in perfect little boxes. I couldn't do it.

Around midnight, I eased out to my car parked near the road and floated, lights off, as quietly as I could until I was almost to Elena's. Then, I hammered it to Cocos International in the fog. I didn't know that the creeping was necessary, but I didn't know it wasn't.

I caught the first red-eye out. It must have been let-the-baggage-boys-fly-the-plane-night at LACSA. The "pilot" doing the honors didn't miss a pothole between San Jose and Miami International.

I'm not a brave flier, and I thought if the terminal wasn't too crowded, I might drop down and kiss the ratty carpet when we disembarked. No way was I getting back on that plane for the Orlando leg. I grabbed a rental, one of those imitation cars about the size and color of a jelly bean, and stopped at the first hotel I came to. I needed some sleep and some time to sort.

Lying in bed, wired on stale adrenaline, a cactus growing in my mouth, I kept coming back full circle to where I started.

Idiot logic dictated that this thing was close in to Ike Pike, but I couldn't spot the keyhole. Every time I'd run a maybe by, I'd hit a rubber wall. Motive.

I couldn't convince myself that any of the outstanding candidates would have sufficient cause to justify the possible consequences. The old man had way too much to lose. Besides, Ezekiel Pike would have gotten over what I considered the worst hurdle long ago: accepting the fact that his son was gay. But who knows how a guy with that much power might react to a greedy little fuck like Manny Quesada?

Steve Glass came on tough, but not in a way that would make me believe he'd kill someone. The besides on this one: despite our little last tag episode at Elena's, he was probably an okay guy. He was very protective of Ike and that was cool, too. No, Steve Glass might jump in your shit, might even slip you a sucker punch if you pushed hard enough, but he wouldn't kill you. I didn't think.

Then the sister. Unless God had given her personal instruction, I couldn't see that going anywhere, either. I did wonder if Carla Pike Parrant was capable of mustering up a prayer for an unborn niece floating in the belly of a titty dancer who would be strutting her stuff somewhere up or down Orange Blossom Trail. I figured Carla was pro-life; I wondered where she stood on this one.

Sis's moral predicament seemed so De Sadian in such an asexual way it made me want to laugh, so I did.

I flashed on myself, a sleep-deprived idiot lying in a hotel room bed, laughing at some pathetic bitch and the sick slice of life that had been carved out for her. I wondered if I should be crying instead of laughing. Atlas had shrugged for me so long ago, I swear I couldn't remember.

I slept.

5

The haul from south Florida to Orlando was no more exciting than I could remember it ever being. Just a long concrete drag dotted with the chronic collection of gas stations, roadside restaurants, a few slash pines, and the backsides of mud-colored houses making up the endless string of "subdivisions." And then the occasional black-and-tan sitting in an obvious spot, keeping the flow down to about ten over the limit.

I traded the jelly bean for my own car at Orlando International about two and headed over to Orange Blossom Trail. I needed to call Jay Feingle in St. Paul, and I needed a hit from Orange County's vital stats to see if Crystal Johnston maybe had parents. More urgent would be the fading memory of the staff of the Hio Motel.

The Hio jutted back ten or twelve units on each side, six across the back to perfect the U. The place was painted so pink it would have made a flamingo blush. There once was an overhang, but it had probably been pulled down by so many drunks so many times someone had said fuck it and put up a smaller version, no posts.

I knew the place by another name. This used to be the Ohio,

but the new owner had knocked out the neon outline of the first O and put the Pepto pink paint in its place. You could still see that it once said *Ohio*. Bang, bang; brush, brush; now you're the Hio.

The iodine tang of curry was such an overwhelming part of the lobby, it was nearly everything. I remember a counter, a couple of blue chairs, a rubber tree plant that I don't think was real, and that smell.

A round and brown woman with a dot and a sari sang out cheerfully when I came in, but her eyes were saying I wasn't standard traffic.

"May I help you, sir?" All the emphasis was on *help*.

I found my wallet and handed her a card that had my name on it. Under my name it said CRISIS ABATEMENT, and there were some dead phone numbers at the bottom.

The woman looked at it like it might be antimatter, flipped it over, flipped it back, and got considerably cooler. "What you want?"

I pulled out a smile, a door to door salesman's model, and the picture of the girl. I laid the latter on the counter, tapped it with a fingernail, and said, "I'm looking for this young lady. Word is she stayed here recently."

Her look went from cool to guarded. Over her shoulder, she yelled for someone named Hamid. There was more, but that's all I could keep up with.

A dark man appeared in the doorway behind her. He wore the same guarded expression as the woman and a hammerless .38 in his belt. His face said he really wished I wasn't standing there.

He and the woman spoke in their sing-song for a bit, while he glanced at the picture, glanced at me then back to the picture. He put a hand, palm down, on the photo and began saying, "No. No. We have no seen this person."

There were only the three of us in the lobby; if the guy was

24

looking for someone who believed him, we'd have to make it a foursome.

I grinned, said, "Come on. Of course you have. She stayed here weekend before last."

"No. Not this person. We have no seen this person."

The woman took a turn. "Why you want this girl?"

The man shoved her aside with, "Are you police? If you are police, you must say. Law is this way. If you are police, you must say."

I was getting good entertainment value out of this, considering what it had cost me so far, but we needed to move on. "No. I'm not police."

The guy made a wimpy sound through pouty lips but seemed to ease down some.

"I'm working for her parents. They retained me to track her down."

The man relaxed a little more, but the woman's eyebrows went up. A smile showed up for her face. "Her parens, huh?"

"Yeah." Once again someone was lying, and no one believed it.

The woman shook her head, still smiling a little, shrugged out, "Yeah. She stay four days. Trouble. Much trouble."

The man said something and I could tell by the tone it was a warning. She scolded back and he shrugged.

"Much trouble. Much drinking and men. Too much trouble."

"Like stolen credit cards?"

She went guarded again. "We only find later, credit card no good. She hold room on one credit card, then she check out with other card, no good one."

The lady frankly didn't give a damn. The credit card company would still foot the bill. There was something soft in that direction so I pushed that way a little. "The card didn't come up stolen? No hold or anything?"

The man spoke in the mother tongue, then she said, "The machine. Is no working that night. No verification."

I sat on that with a grin wide enough to make the rest of the room fidget. "You should have that other credit card number, right? The one she was holding the room with?"

The woman's turn to be unbelievable: "No. Maybe we throw it out."

"Maybe you don't. Maybe you think if the one card was stolen, then this one might be, too, just hadn't been discovered missing and reported. Maybe you guys did a little shopping yourselves."

That got me more mother tongue action.

The man was going red in the face again. He shouted, "You go! You go now!"

I smiled nice for him.

"This my motel. You go now!"

His diction wasn't getting any better either. "That credit card number." My hand was out.

More mother tongue; the man flapped at me with both hands and disappeared; the woman dug in a drawer.

She laid the imprinted merchant copy on the counter and looked hard in my eyes. "You are not talking to anyone? About this?"

"No. No one you would be concerned with. Thanks." I threw a couple of twenties on the counter and picked up the imprint.

The woman palmed the two bills, bent them twice, and they disappeared into the folds of the sari. She was smiling again. "You no work for the parens."

"No?"

"No." Her head shook. "The parens, they come here one night."

"Nice folks?"

She put a nasty laugh on that. "Yes, very nice. We must have police here. The father is very drunk. He want to fight every-

26

one." She shrugged. "Hamid no like police here, but . . . sometimes, maybe better, huh?"

"Yeah. They lock him up?"

The woman shrugged for me again. "This I do not know. He ride away with them. In the back of the car, with, how do you say . . . ?" She made circles around her wrists with her fingers.

I said, "Handcuffs." She nodded. "What day was this?"

Her brown face turned to the ceiling, "Tuesday. Last, not this. Maybe Wednesday, but I think Tuesday."

I threw another twenty and a card with pertinent phone numbers on the counter, winked, and said, "You see her, it's worth a C-note to me."

"*C* means what? One hundred?"

"Yeah."

"I will call." She was looking at the new card.

I crossed the asphalt mosaic that was the parking lot, grabbed my door handle, paused, spun around.

The sun so bright, the building so pink, the glare almost knocked the breath out of me. I went back to the door and stuck my head into the aroma. My Indian princess was smiling.

"Listen," I said, "it's worth a grand, you put me in front of this girl."

Her three eyes studied me. "*Grand* means one thousand?"

"Yeah."

She gave me back my wink, said, "Okay, buddy."

I threw her a wave and stepped back into the heat. No doubt, I'd be hearing from Madam Curry.

A real shower and a change of clothes that hadn't spent several days in a suitcase lay north. Raleigh Lightstep and central booking were south. If Raleigh was in a decent mood, I could get a short list on who went to jail Tuesday and Wednesday last. If he wasn't in a good mood, that lead was fucked. Raleigh wasn't known for good moods.

Vital statistics was east, but without a court order, I could spend an hour leaning on a shiny new wooden counter at the shiny new concrete courthouse downtown. I could lie, aw shucks, finesse my ass off, and probably ride down to street level in a shiny new steel elevator without so much as a social on Crystal Gail Johnston. Records people had gotten real funny over the past several years, and palm grease in the wrong palm downtown could put me in another federal program for a few years. I did have another option, but I hadn't made up my mind to utilize that avenue yet. I knew I would though.

Raleigh worked the swing shift, so he would only have been at work for an hour or so. He'd be doing dinner around seven or eight, and that was my in. The man had a demonstrated weakness for Chinese food. I could call from my place, he'd ask what the fuck I wanted, I'd say I smelled Chinese. If he was in a bad mood, I'd get a disconnect click. If he was in a good mood, he'd ask what the fuck I wanted again, I'd tell him, he'd do a nasty snort for a laugh and say he hadn't noticed my signature on his paycheck, so why the fuck did I think he worked for me. I'd ignore the question and ask when was the last time he watched a Magic game from a box, and Raleigh would name a restaurant. It wouldn't be the China Ho Express either. The food may or may not be decent, but you could bet your ass it would be spendy.

It sounded like I had convinced myself to head for home, so I crossed the two southbound lanes, squatted in the turn lane for a few, and punched north. I was at the little apartment that doubles as my office in less than fifteen.

Possibly, the only thing worse than leaving the iron on and burning your place down when you go away is forgetting to take the garbage out before you leave. Luckily for the wildlife in the trash bin, I had remembered to put the AC up to about eighty. It seemed like they had appreciated the gesture. The smell was only slightly worse than the county landfill.

I raised the windows, all three of them, and left the door open after I sat the trash outside. The impatient little light on my message machine was begging for attention. Nothing exciting. Jay Feingle had called, left a number that was long distance enough I didn't recognize the area code.

My ex had called with some bullshit explaining why she was going to fuck me out of my next weekend visitation with my kid. I listened and was again reminded of what a master at the art of passing off rat shit for raisins this woman was.

There is a curse I reserve for special occasions. I used it, stripped to the skin, and stood under a hot shower for a very long time.

When the hot was gone from the shower, one part of me still quietly cursed but the other parts felt better.

I toweled off on the way to the kitchen, found a forgotten Newcastle Brown in the fridge, and went back into the bedroom to dress.

I put on a light cotton pullover with short sleeves and a V neck, tucked it into experienced jeans, stuck Cole-Haan ankle boots on the ends of my legs, grabbed my beer and a cordless phone, and went out to my garden.

A dozen hits on redial and a ten-minute wait got me Raleigh Lightstep. We had the conversation pretty much as predicted until we got to the Magic part.

When I mentioned the box seats, Raleigh threw me a change up. "Who give a fuck about the Magic anymore?"

I wasn't the one to be asking, and I reminded Raleigh of it.

"Oh yeah. That's right. You the motherfucker buys a box every year, don't give a fuck about the game."

"That would be me."

"Why you do that?"

"Think about it, Raleigh."

He did, then said, "You know Luther Vandross playin' at the House of Blues in a couple of weeks?"

"I can't recall ever giving a shit where Luther Vandross might be."

"Uh huh. I got a feelin' you about to get interested. Pretty quick, too, 'fore all the good seats is gone. What you think, Sloan?"

I was thinking he was right. "Center, close in as available?"

"You got it, dog. Look here, I'll be seein' you." Someone had come into the office with Raleigh. "Yeah, yeah." Pause, then, "You know that's right," going real black with it.

"Your boss standing there?"

"Uh huh. You could say that. Look here, I'm gone have to slide, finish up what I'm doin' so I can get outta here for dinner about seven-thirty." He paused; I hadn't said a word. "Yeah." Pause. "Yeah." Pause. "I think I'm gone try that new place on I Drive. Yeah, that's the one. What you say it was?" Another pause. "Splendid Panda? Uh huh."

"Nice and fucking expensive, Raleigh?"

"Oh yeah. But that ain't no problem for you, dog. Hey, I'll talk with you later on." Click.

Sounded like a date. I was glad Raleigh was in a good mood. Sometimes it's hard to tell.

I called HoB and used my credit card to put two tickets on hold for Raleigh Lightstep, three back, dead middle. It set me back $37.50 a pop. Put a fifty, sixty-dollar dinner on that, it should get me a short list of white guys to chat up tomorrow.

I tried punching another number up from memory, got no further than that irritating four-tone sequence that says try it again. My address book knew the number by heart. I went in and got it, redialed.

Ring.

Ring.

Ring.

"Hello?" A woman's voice.

"Is this one-nine hundred-do-me?"

"Mmm. Talk dirty to me, firm and virile man." The voice was low now, husky, wanting.

"You know what I'd like to do to you, lady?"

"Yeah. I was there while you were doing it last time, remember?" The torchiness had gone back to friendly.

"Well, maybe I wanta do it again."

"No you don't, Sloan. I'm over here sitting on it, and you never come by and push me over to even look at it."

I didn't know where to go next, so I stayed with the playful thing. "How about I come over this evening?"

"And what? Ravish me?"

"Yeah."

"Which part, Sloan?" Her mood was getting cooler.

"Which part do you think?"

"My mind. You need something, don't you?"

"Nothing somebody with a red hot modem and a smooth stroke on the keyboard couldn't cure."

There was something like a faint sigh, then, "That's exactly what I thought. What time?"

"Nine sound good?"

"Sure." It wasn't enthusiastic.

There was an uncomfortable little silence that I broke with, "Look, Nat, I—"

"Can it, Sloan. It's my problem, okay? I don't know why I keep doing this to myself. I'm okay; you're okay; together we suck." Natalie gave me a few seconds with that, then said, "Besides that, you're too damned old for me. See you at ten." Click.

I held the phone in both hands, looking at it like it was Natalie's face. "Goddamn, girl. You scare the hell out of me. You know that?"

Natalie Poe was a damned decent representative of the female race. Way more female than I would ever deserve. Bobbed hair the color and texture of new corn silks, high cheekbones, full, almost pouty lips, breasts made in heaven by someone with big hands, hips as narrow as a schoolgirl's, and legs longer than a Baptist sermon. More brains on one side than I probably had in my entire shit-packed head. Pliable and acrobatic under the blanket. Adventurous and precocious everywhere.

There were down strokes. She could be a class-A bitch. That made her a prime candidate for a future ex-wife. That was something I was trying to avoid like I would avoid the mumps at my age. She was several years younger than I was, and sometimes I was conceited enough to feel embarrassed that it seemed too easy to take advantage of her. Then some days, I had felt like I was the pigeon.

Whatever had gone on between us had gone to sleep two years ago but it hadn't died and it wasn't over. And maybe that's what scared me the most. That and the fact that her clock was banging like a square wheel.

Dueling neon made it tougher to find the Splendid Panda than I had been led to believe by the genuine Asian voice when I called for directions. I found it nestled in a strip plaza with the obligatory discount shoe outlet, a yogurt shop, and a puppy mill.

The shoe outlet I understood. The yogurt shop, with the cutsie extra *p* and an *e*, made good business sense here in touro world. The puppy mill escaped me.

I grabbed a good parking spot, crossed some concrete, went through some glass, and found Raleigh Lightstep halfway through a Tsingtao. He was at a table with glass over a red table cloth over a white table cloth, all turned forty-five degrees to the other.

The walls were a different red and Buddha on a shelf by a fountain was another red. There was a red and gold mural dittoing around the room with Buddha, white-faced and saggy-breasted, repeating himself dozens of times among nubile Chinese girls with pert breasts and caramel-colored faces.

"The fuck you been?" was all the greeting I would get.

"What? Am I late?"

"You always late."

Even sitting, Raleigh was a head higher than anyone else in the room. The ugly green double-knit county uniform was losing the battle to bag him.

Raleigh was a little heavier, a little softer in spots than he was five years back when another county detective popped him in the knee at a cluster-fucked dope raid. He limped a little, he moved a little slower, and he had lost just a tad of the intensity twelve years with the DUKE boys, the sheriff's neo-fascist drug squad, had cooked into him. All that considered, sitting there, he still looked like someone only a full-blown loon would dick with. Cool, muddy eyes set in a wide muddy face that had *don't fuck with me* written all over it, and all that sitting on a fifty-five gallon drum. That was Raleigh Lightstep.

I dug in my jeans and came out with an orange Post-it. There was a number written on it. I shoved it across to Raleigh. He looked at it like he was insulted that I should offer him something so blithe.

"What's this? Your momma's phone number?"

I was saved from having to produce a snappy comeback by a girl with a cheongsam and very pale skin. She was about as Chinese as Raleigh or me. She took my request for two more Tsingtao beers and a big order of hot and sour soup. Raleigh wouldn't have waited on me to order. I didn't have to ask. I knew Raleigh.

When the waitress had cleared, Raleigh said, "I ran white guys, thirty and up, picked up by the city Tuesday noon through Thursday noon. That cover your man?"

"Fuck, I hope so. How many souls?"

"Fifty or so."

I rolled my eyes at the tally and Raleigh said, "Goddam, Sloan, whatcha want? Me to call the motherfuckers, ask 'em who got picked up at the Hio Motel? Shit, half won't even remember bein' picked up, the other half ain't gone talk about it. You probably wastin' your precious resources, dog." He gave me one of his rare grins, put the Post-it with his House of Blues confirmation number on it in a shirt pocket. "But I do appreciate your appreciation."

"Yeah. Tell Luther I said hey. Two weeks, I'll probably still be running this fucking list."

"You gone cry, what the baby gone do?"

The non-Chinese waitress brought our beers and a poo poo platter. She lit the sterno and put a little plate in front of each of us.

Raleigh grabbed my plate, shoved it back at the girl, and said, "He ain't gone be eatin' none of this. He want somethin', he need to order it."

The waitress looked at me funny, eyebrows arched high. I grinned and said, "I'm fine. Just soup for me, please. I'm the one who has to pick up the tab for what party of four over there eats." The girl walked away, but she didn't get it. I'm not sure I did.

Between a strip of satay and a fried dumpling, Raleigh straightened a leg, pried a twice-folded printout from a pants pocket. He tossed the wad on the table, watched me for a while, then said, "You gone look?"

I gave him a shrug, put a leg on a knee. "Later."

Raleigh had a chicken drummette; now he had a chicken

bone. Around the mouthful of meat, he said, "Second page. One up from the bottom. What's his name?"

I looked. A little pencil mark was beside a name. The name was Donnie Ray Hatcher. I said it.

"Yeah." Raleigh made a face at what he was eating. "The fuck is that gummy shit?"

"Octopus."

That made Raleigh grunt. "They two of 'em. You want the other one?" He was holding a skewer with a blob on it in my direction.

"Nah. I want something, I'll order it."

That got me a mean look from muddy eyes and a point with the skewer. "Donnie Ray. How come redneck white guys like to use two front names?"

I shrugged for him.

"Anyhow, that's your man."

"How did you get there?"

"Read it and weep. Forty-six. He live out toward Bithlo. He got picked up D and D. Had him a glass pipe in his pocket. Did him a little resisting dance with the boys picked him up."

"Well, shit, maybe I should drop everything and run on out there now. Goddamn, Raleigh, detective work like that, it's a wonder you're not teaching criminal justice out at the community college."

Raleigh looked tired for me. "Try this then, Sherlock. The man been a guest six times in the last two years. Five times, he sit till he see the judge. This time, he out soon as Fat Tommy get his round little bail-bondin' ass over to Thirty-third Street."

He got my attention. It was a good point and I put it where it belonged. I scanned the list. "No Johnstons." I had been stuck on finding a Johnston.

"Why the fuck you think 'cause the girl named Johnston, the man gotta be named Johnston?"

"Wishful thinking."

"Yeah, well it's a mixed-up world, dog. Look at me and you. All the talent I got, and me sittin' at a desk, tellin' the loved ones of lowlifes what it's gone take to get they garbage home; and you, the god-awful lack of talent you got at the same thing, and you makin' it hand over, dog. Makin' it hand over."

"You see our waitress, ask her if she could maybe bring some extra napkins over. I always feel a good cry coming on when you talk that way."

6

Natalie Poe's parents had an oops. He was eighteen years old now and his name was Maxwell.

Maxwell didn't like me. He had never liked me and had gone to great lengths not to hide his dislike. When he was sixteen, he took a swing at me and about halfway through it, I swept his feet and dropped him like a sack of coal. He'd never forgiven me, and I had not put my back to him since.

He answered the door at Nat's. He leaned back, pushed his chest out, pushed his bottom lip out. I guess he was going for tough; he wasn't making it. He said, "Whatcha need?"

I brushed by him, and said, "A little space."

He followed me in and I turned my head enough to keep his big ass in my peripheral.

"You weren't invited in yet, bastard."

"Nice talk. They teach you that at that preppy little institute of the elite you go to?"

"Listen, dick breath, I'm not some little punk you can kick around anymore."

I stopped, turned, got right in Maxwell's face. "Yes you are,

Maxie. You may be a little taller, a little fatter, but you're still just a chubby, rich boy punk, and I hope to God you grow out of it before you hit drinking age."

"Yeah? Why's that, jerk wad?"

"So I don't have to beat the living fuck out of you for using so much schoolyard French."

Natalie came through a door smiling. "Boys, boys."

I turned to look. I hadn't seen her in two months and the punk could have detached my retina and I'd have never seen it coming.

Maxwell and I went to our respective corners, Maxwell glaring at me, me ogling his sister.

The sister must have liked the ogling. She sent Maxwell on his way.

I planted myself on a long chair that probably had a name like divan or chesterfield. Like most everything else in the room, it was white. I'd say white, but someone more erudite might have a more exciting name for it.

There was some abstract shit in primary colors on the white walls here and there. A couple of statues, also white. Besides that, there was leather, glass, chrome, and some light-colored wood, but not much of it. The minimalism was lost on me. I like clutter.

Natalie went out, came back with a brown beer and some sort of wine cooler, held the wine cooler out, "You want?" She was pulling my leg and we smiled.

"No. The beer's fine."

The beer was offered and I took it. "No glass?"

"No glass."

Natalie sat on the end of the long chair, legs the opposite direction to mine. "So, how have you been, Sloan?"

"Good, good. You?"

"Same. Good. How's business?"

"Good. Yours?"

"Good. Busy."

Some silence.

"Should we talk about the weather?"

That got a grin out of her. "Who are we kidding?"

"Not me."

"You horny?"

"You bet." I could have told her she would make a eunuch go bony, but I didn't.

"You want to work first or fuck first?"

I loved it when she talked that way. I thought about it. "Since we can't do both at once . . ."

"Not that we haven't tried."

I conceded the point. "And the latter, hopefully, will go longer than the former, I say we do the suggested activities in the suggested order."

"Sounds like a plan. Bring your beer this way, please."

I did. Down a hall, through the bedroom and its nice familiar smell, into a dressing room that had lost its identity to cyber trends.

I can put out a decent letter on Works. I can even bludgeon Quick Books Pro into giving me an invoice when necessity dictates. Beyond that—well, there's nothing beyond that. Computers aren't my thing. A victim of the digital divide.

Computers were Natalie Poe's thing. She taught the stuff at UCF. Being head of the computer science department, I guess she actually didn't teach anymore. I didn't really know what Natalie did at the University, and I guess that was a statement about me and relationships that wasn't too flattering.

It took her longer to fire up the machinery than it did for her to get me a birth certificate and a social security number on Ms. Crystal Gail Johnston.

I read the names: Joy Marie and Gary James Johnston. No news really, but a bingo on the address. I went in my pocket.

"What's that say, babe? The address on the proud parents?"

"One thirty-one Crossover Road, lot number seven, Bithlo, Florida."

I snapped the back of a finger on the sheet Raleigh had given me. "Son of a bitch, Raleigh. Step-daddy."

Natalie wrinkled her forehead.

"Raleigh said this was my man. Picked him off the list. Damned if he wasn't dead-on. Thank you, Raleigh."

Natalie crossed her arms and put on a pouty face. "So all the kudos go to crazy Raleigh, huh?"

I smiled, put my hands out palms up, feigning innocence.

"Okay, hotshot, I raise Raleigh a blow job and see him breakfast in the morning."

"That's not how you bet. You have to see him something, then raise him something."

"Well, that's how I'm betting." She was making promises with her eyes that I'd hold her to later. "So who wins this round?"

"You, of course."

"You're smarter than you look, big guy."

"So I've been told."

Natalie killed her equipment, crooked a finger at me, and went into the bedroom. I was seeing an increasing expanse of bare skin as she lost her clothes on the way.

By the time she was to the bed, she was nude. She lay on the bed, on her back. Looking at me over the soft geography of her body, the easy rises and nice turns, the fuzzy secrets which I knew a little about, she said, "Where the hell have you been, Duncan?"

I shrugged. "Nowhere, baby. Absolutely nowhere."

7

Natalie reneged on the promised breakfast, substituting a cup of Cuban coffee and another bounce on the bed. I felt like I still got the best end of the deal.

When I left, she was on the machine, running the credit card and the social. I'd call later for the hits. I didn't think Crystal would be using her social if she was sincerely on the lam, but I'd bet she was still riding the card, would be until it ran out of gas or bit back.

The East-West Expressway took me nearly to Bithlo. I got off at Highway 50 where the expressway died and went east again.

Junkyard country. Junk cars, junk, tin houses with wheels, fat-bellied goats, and cur dogs. High grass and weeds. Cars on blocks and rusty barbecue grilles. Lumpy dirt roads, pickups, and rednecks. Bithlo, Florida.

A guy at a convenience store put me on Crossover Road. Having a lot number, I had figured the home would be of the mobile variety. I was right.

It was an older job, narrow and long, color nearly gone, but once gold and white. Volunteer lantana was orange and stinky here and there. The grass, what there was of it, appeared to be either crabgrass or sandspur. Without the signature heads, I couldn't tell. It didn't matter anyway. There wasn't enough of it that anyone should really give a shit.

The first step to the beat-up deck was propped up with a cinder block. The second step needed propping up. I stepped over it to the deck.

I knocked on the pebbly surface that was the door. No response. I knocked again. Same response.

I yelled through a void created by a missing jalousie panel. "Donnie Ray. Hey, boy, you home?"

The yell cost me some air. When I replaced it, I got a smell that seemed to end up in the back of my throat. It was a smell I knew. Not quite like shit, not quite like roadkill. It was the smell of the recently dead. My own species.

The knob didn't yield, so I reached in the missing window panel, pushed the burlap weave polyester curtain aside, and flipped the latch. The door swung in on its own, bumped on something wood behind it, and stopped. I put the tail of my shirt over my face in anticipation, and stepped inside.

The smell was worse, but not overwhelming yet. Not like it would be later on, say this evening, after cooking in the not so benevolent Florida sun all day. I used the shirttail to wipe the door latch.

The place was a mess. Cigarette butts spilled out of ashtrays, jack mags and tabloid rags were strewn about with more mundane clutter. The kitchen was worse yet. Dishes piled on sink, stove, and table. There were no more roaches than I would have expected in broad daylight for a place this clean. But nothing stiff.

There was a room off the living room and a hall off the kitchen. I tried the room and found one.

A woman lay on her side in an interpretation of a fetal position, back to me on a bare mattress. Hands bound, feet bound with plastic pull ties, big white ones. Blood had migrated across the ticking around her head, more so at the front. More blowflies at the front also.

I stepped around the bed until I could see the face. Must have been Granny. Most of her forehead was gone. Her eyes were spooked-horse wide, her mouth in a rictus grin. I pushed a foot. She was stiff, eight or ten hours' worth.

I backed out on tiptoe, like I might wake her, and went across the living room and kitchen to the hall. A bedroom on the left was just big enough for a double bed, and that's all that was in it. I passed a washing machine and a place where its companion dryer should have been but wasn't. There was a bathroom on the left also. No one in there but hypersonic cockroaches.

The door at the end of the hall was closed, but the dead smell was stronger. I leaned in the bathroom and grabbed a length of tissue from a roll on the vanity, took some good breaths, turned the knob with the tissue.

The room looked like I would expect Jackson Pollock's workshop to look. A splatterfest of one color: dead red. A fat naked man was on the bed on his back. His hands were under him, feet bound like the woman's in the other room.

If this was Donnie Ray Hatcher, only God knew it. His face was marinara sauce with eyes. Some hand tools were on the bed with him. Somebody had been handy with them.

I looked at the man's body and looked at the tools. A pair of vise grip pliers and shears had been the artist's choice. Pull a plug, snip it off. Pull an appendage, snip it off. I felt a gag rising from down low in my gut and pushed the visual aside.

The second woman, probably Joy Marie, was on her knees in the closet, hands bound behind her, feet bound. She had two long graying braids, and a neat blue-black hole was in the part of her hair low in the back.

I leaned in the closet, but couldn't see much. She had been popped as she lay now. Probably never moved. Just shuddered, bucked against the restraints, pissed herself, and died.

Privacy didn't seem to be an issue for the lucky couple, so I left the door open. I caught myself tiptoeing again going down the hall.

The tissue I had opened the door with had ended up balled in my left fist. I unrolled it, looking for the phone. I hadn't seen one in any of the bedrooms.

I found it on the kitchen wall in an alcove with a stained and dirt-speckled Formica countertop. I lifted the phone with the tissue and punched redial with the back of a fingernail. Second ring: "Hilton, the Corners. How may I direct your call?"

I cradled the phone. My internal warning system didn't like it. Something felt funny about where the redial took me.

I couldn't buy that Crystal would go from the Hio to the Hilton. She wasn't good enough at the credit card game to work it on someone who gave a shit. The Hilton would give a shit.

If it wasn't the girl, then it was a wild card. I didn't want to see a wild card this early in the hand. I guess because I wasn't expecting it yet.

I knew I had to play them like they fell, but I didn't have to like it. I didn't like wild cards, and I didn't like this.

Firing my car up brought out a woman from the double-wide next door who probably validated her life with *Roseanne* show reruns. She had ratty brown hair and an overinflated face, maxed stretch pants, and a halter top. It wasn't a much prettier site than what I had seen over at the Hatchers'.

I gave her a nod that she didn't acknowledge and backed out of lot number seven. The curse that was blossoming on my lips fell over to full bloom when I found her in the rearview mouthing my tag number. She disappeared inside.

The woman had made me. Now, I had to make something. It's called a decision.

I didn't like cops. Raleigh Lightstep was as near to an exception as I had ever made. I also didn't like the idea of whackadoodles running around my town snipping chunks off the citizenry and head popping them. My concern was probably selfishly motivated, considering the next trim job could be on me.

I was on the horns. Dump it, damn it.

Cell phone: Two rings later. "Yeah."

"Raleigh."

Silence.

"Raleigh." Me again.

"The fuck you want?"

"Advice."

"Bullshit." Click.

Five rings.

"This best not be no fuckin' Sloan."

"What if it had been your mother?"

Click.

I threw a *goddamn* at the windshield and dialed again, ready. There was a break in the line but no one spoke. I said, "Three down at Donnie Ray's."

Silence until I said, "Raleigh?"

Hard exhale. "Why the fuck you do this to me? Huh? Like I ain't got my own shit to deal with. Like I need some cracker motherfucker callin' me with shit like this. Whatchu think I am, Sloan, some dial-up shrink show on AM radio? Man, I don't fuckin' believe your ass."

I put the one on Raleigh he always puts on me when I'm whining. "You gonna cry, what's the baby gonna do?"

Raleigh puffed hard a couple of times. I was glad I wasn't standing in front of him. "Where they at? That Bithlo address?"

"Yeah."

"Knowin' you ain't called it in."

"No."

"Goddam, Sloan."

"Hey, I'm calling it in now. To you."

"To me?" Raleigh's voice had gone up high, looking for incredulous.

Next, I got called a motherfucker again and hung up on.

It's really hard to tail someone on a modern six lane without being spotted. It's even harder on a road like the expressway. Not enough traffic between rushes.

I had seen the Buick before, enough to mark it. There it was again, a couple of rises back, holding off.

At the toll plaza, I whipped in the employee parking area and jumped out. My shirttail was out, my hand was on the butt of a 9-millimeter Smith stuck in the waist band of my jeans. I walked quickly toward the toll booths.

The brown Buick spotted me, rolled left, and blew through the E-Pass lane at about seventy. There were two birds in the front. The one on my side, the passenger side, turned his head and put a hand up to cover his face. The driver was a Latino I didn't know.

I ran back to my car and jammed out of the parking area, lost traction at the toll booth, and boosted it up to about ninety. The Buick was half a mile ahead and moving pretty well.

I punched another twenty miles an hour into the speedometer. I was gaining on them when I heard a not so unfamiliar sound, found it in my rearview. Florida Highway Patrol.

That cost Ike Pike $280 and cost me a look at that wild card.

8

The electronic voice of my message machine told me I had seven messages.

The first message was Madam Curry from the Hio Motel. "Mr. Sloan, this is . . ." I have no earthly idea what she said her name was, too consonant intensive, "at the Hio Motel. Two two six zero South Orange Blossom Trail, Orlando, Florida. I have some information for you that is worthy." She left a number.

Second: Jay Feingle. Jay had lost some southern texture from his voice up in St. Paul, but he was still an asshole. "Duncan, Jay Feingle. Uh . . . love to hear something from you. This is my second message. I thought we would be in tighter contact. Uh . . . to be honest, I'm not real happy. Uh . . . how about trying to return a call now and again? As soon as you get this message, you need to call my office."

"Yes sir, Mr. Feingle. Right away, Mr. Feingle." I was talking to myself.

Third: Madam Curry again. Still didn't catch her real name.

Fourth: Ike Pike. Please call. I'm headed out of town. I got another letter.

Fifth: Madam Curry once again. She was telling me it was tomorrow now.

Sixth: A low feminine moany voice going over to a near growl way back in someone's throat. Natalie's. "Oh, hey, Sloan. Just thinking about you. Really about last night. Got four or five good hits on the card. Nothing on the kid's social, though. A P.S. on the credit card: it's been pulled. Reported missing yesterday." A hesitation, then less business, more personal, "Please call me."

"Jesus, Nat." I was talking to myself again.

And lucky number seven? Yeah, Madam Curry again. This time she tried chumming the waters a little. "Now there are two come by. Asking, Mr. Sloan. Asking like you are asking."

The phone rang. I had a good idea who it might be. I answered, "Hio Motel. How may I direct your call?"

After a short hesitation, "How do you know it is me?"

"Just a hunch."

"What is hunch?"

I passed. "What's up?"

"You should come to see me. I have things to tell."

Things to tell; things to sell. "You see the girl?"

"Umm . . . no, but I have something else."

"Guys coming by?"

She was thinking, maybe trying to remember what she had used for chum. "Yes. Now, today, this morning, one more come."

"Who were they?"

"I have a card from him."

"What's it say? Read it to me." I was having fun. No way was she going to tell me over the phone.

"No. You must come here. Your language, maybe I do not have it so good, huh?"

She seemed to be doing okay with the language to me. It looked like she was about to parlay the sixty I had already given her into a hundred or better.

"Okay, ma'am. I'll swing by in a bit."

"Hey, you talk to me, okeh? Not to my husband, okeh?"

"Okay."

"When you come?"

"In a bit."

"You hurry, okeh?"

"Yeah." I cut the connection.

Jay Feingle's number got me a promise from a cheery-sounding young lady to tell him I'd called. Could she have my number? I told her she had it. How about a cell phone number, could she have that? No.

Nat's number at work got me a trip into voice mail. I mimicked her moany groany, said, "Just thinking about you thinking about me. If you don't get me here, try my cell." Out of past habit, I was about to toss a "luv ya" in, caught it clumsily, and remolded it to, "Later."

I felt a little stupid for it and couldn't or wouldn't put a finger on why. I buried it so it wouldn't distract me. That's what I told myself.

Another chipper, clipped Yankee voice asked if I would like to hold when I told her my name and asked for Pike. I told her I'd love to be put on hold. I had understood the contact number Pike had left me with was direct. Maybe I was wrong.

Instead of the anticipated Pike, I got another feminine voice, this one fairly unchipper, no-bullshit professional. She said she was Donna, Pike's personal something. I wasn't paying much attention to that part.

"Mr. Sloan. Glad you called. How are you?"

I could tell by her voice, she didn't give a shit how I was but felt a professional compulsion to ask. "Fine, thanks. Ike around?"

"No. Mr. Pike is in Orlando by now. He placed a call to you last evening to inform you. I have a number for you."

"Shoot."

"He is in room six eleven at the Hilton. Let me see."

I could hear office debris being shuffled. "Four Corners?"

"Yes. That's it. Okay, I have the number." She gave it to me. It went well with the cool zip moving up my spine.

We bid each other a warm and insincere farewell and I sat staring at the opposite wall for a while. A bell was going off in the back of my head. I was wishing it was clearer.

The switchboard at the Hilton passed me to yet another cheery, clipped Yankee voice. Steve Glass.

I told him who it was, lost the cheery, but got Pike.

"Hey, Duncan. How goes it?"

"Slow. Progress, but slow."

"Well, that's not all bad. What I had in mind was meeting here this evening. We can have dinner brought up and go over whatever it is we have to go over. That work?"

"Yeah. Where's Jay Feingle?"

"He'll be here. He's in Miami with my sister, Carla. She's taking over some TV ministry down there, and Jay's working the security stuff for her."

We agreed on eight o'clock and signed off. The bell was still ringing in my head.

Paulie Mopps is a damn good trial lawyer. He has an office on Livingston that usually doesn't smell any worse than a muck shoe full of shit. Also, he's very short, maybe five feet, even with the double-decker stacked heels he wears.

Paulie doesn't spend a lot of time in court. It seems that even if you're a damn good criminal lawyer, being a midget makes it hard to get taken seriously. And, I know referring to someone as a midget isn't exactly on the cutting edge of the sensitivity movement, but I've always thought of Paulie as a midget. Sue me.

Besides the obvious distinctions of legal wizardry, Worst Office Odor award five years running, and being able to hide in carry-on luggage, Paulie Mopps has another gift. The man is a walking who's who on the titty bar scene. A mole two inches to the right of the left nipple? Paulie can put a stage name with the description and probably come up with the name the lady was born with. He's that good. If that's considered being good.

I didn't know if Crystal was dancing if, indeed, Pike's spawn was swelling in her belly, but if she was, Paulie would be the man to ask. I called him.

"Paul C. Mopps."

"Paulie."

"Sloan? Is this Duncan Sloan? Calling me? Excuse me while I fall to my knees and give thanks."

"Fuck you, Paulie."

"You talk like that to someone you need a favor out of?"

"Who says I need a favor? Maybe I just miss your toxic wit."

"Ha. I'm sitting here trying to conjure up a scenario where Duncan Sloan calls anybody, and I mean anybody, where he wouldn't want something. Know what?"

"Yeah. You can't do it."

"You know the man."

We laughed some on my tab, then Paulie said, "What's up? What do you need?"

"Seen anybody with a tattoo in your latest travels?"

"Why, heavens no. The girls I associate with would never resort to such tawdry behavior. What's it look like?"

"An eyeball with wings."

"Left cheek. High up, almost to the hip? Wings of blue? Little skinny blonde thing. No tits. Does a jailbait routine?"

"Sounds right."

"Haven't seen her."

"Give it, Paulie."

"What's the payout?"

"It's always about money with you, isn't it, Paulie?"

"Yes, it is."

51

"A bill for a lead, a yard on an introduction."

"You owe me a hundred bucks."

"Where is she?"

"Don't know."

"Then how do you get I owe you the hundred?"

"Know where she was. She's gone now."

"When?"

"Oh, a week or so back."

"She look pregnant?"

"There's the off chance that I wasn't looking at her stomach."

"Don't you think you would have noticed?"

"Maybe. Still worth that bill?"

"Yeah, sure. Where?"

"The Sugar Shack. Know it?"

"No."

"Try the Trail, just south of Gore Street. Damn, Sloan, you don't get out much nowadays, huh?"

"Paulie, I don't see where not knowing the location of every coochie joint in town exactly makes me a recluse."

"Uh huh. Then when was the last time you went out? Socially, I mean."

"Don't work it so hard, Paulie. It'll give you a stroke."

"How about that brainy blonde, the one with the chest and the waif look. The schoolmarm? When's the last time you saw her?"

"Last night."

"Dinner and a movie? Or just a biological visit to loinville?"

I was embarrassed to say I'd used business as the excuse. "Whatcha doing, Paulie, going into the advice racket? Or maybe you're gonna write a book about how all your full-size friends can get laid and you can't?"

Paulie started laughing. "Ah, I love it, Sloan. You're so damned cool, Mr. Laidback, till someone kicks you where you flinch. Then, man, do you go nasty. You ever notice that about you, Sloan?"

"Thanks, Paulie. I'll send you an extra fifty for the enlightenment session. You see her again, you posthaste me."

"For a grand? I'll bring her over to your place. See you, Sloan."

"Yeah." I killed the phone.

That was about as far as Ma Bell could take me for right now, and I was curious about who'd been by to see Madam Curry. It wouldn't mean much now, but maybe later it might help sort the good guys from the bad guys. Who knows?

I hadn't had anything since coffee at Nat's and should have been fairly famished after the acrobatics at her place, but one look in the fridge was all the lunch I needed. Shit, after the scene at Donnie Ray's, I might never eat again.

9

I was sitting at the light at Country Club and Orange Blossom Trail when my cell went off. The phone had rolled off the passenger seat and I had to unbuckle to get at it.

"Yeah."

"You need to go your ass back out to Bithlo." It was Raleigh. He didn't sound as happy as he ordinarily was.

I didn't know what to say so I gave him some quiet.

"You got that, didn't you?"

"Yeah. Thanks, Raleigh."

"Thanks, Raleigh? Fuck you, Sloan. The hell you expect? What I'm supposed to say? Yeah, some anonymous wrong number call me, told me they three dead crackers at a trailer house in Bithlo."

"Who'd you call?"

"Why you care? Don't none of 'em like you, no how."

"Who was it?"

"Booker."

"Aw fuck, Raleigh."

"Booker ain't that bad."

"Yeah. Maybe to you. He likes your ass."

"Shit. Booker don't like nobody."

"I'm taking comfort in that."

I think Raleigh was laughing. I couldn't recall ever hearing him laugh, so I wasn't sure. "Hey, Sloan, you the one called needin' advice, wasn't you?"

"I thought that's what I was doing."

"Well, here, let me help you out. Go your ass back out to trailer park country and take your licks."

I said thanks again, but Raleigh was gone.

There was a white unmarked at lot number seven when I got back out there. A man in a dark blue T-shirt with SHERIFF'S DEPARTMENT in white lettering was talking on a phone, leaning on the car. He was big enough to rent himself out as a shade tree.

He saw me and motioned me to park behind him. The cop finished his conversation, pushed a button, and yelled, "Miz Colley."

The dough woman from the double-wide stepped out to a better deck than the one at lot seven. The cop said, "He the one?"

She looked tough at me, squinting, scowling, ready to convict. "Yeah. That's him."

"Thanks, ma'am. You can go back inside now."

"What the hell's goin' on over there?"

"We gone have us a look and see."

"You done had a look."

"Yeah. That's right, ma'am. You need to go on back in."

A pale, skinny man, bald, about half the woman's weight, barefoot, can of beer, stepped out behind the woman. "Hey, I don't care for niggers tellin' my old lady what she needs or don't need."

Lt. Det. Mose Booker put a pair of jet black eyes on the man. "Right now, see, you ain't lookin' at no nigger, rube. You lookin' at a deputy sheriff. You and the missus need to step inside."

"And what if we don't?" The woman stepped back in.

"Then I'm gone handcuff your skinny white ass and put you in the trunk of this car right here." Booker patted a fender tenderly.

"You better watch that mouth, boy. I got friends with the department my own self."

"Good. When we get back to Thirty-third Street, they'll be somebody to scrape what's left of your sorry ass outta my trunk."

Booker hitched the phone under a couple of rolls of flab and took two long strides toward the double-wide. The redneck got off a few interesting epithets before he allowed Roseanne to drag him inside.

When Booker turned, I had a sick smile on my face. I could guess how it was going to go after that.

"Knowed it was you."

I held tight.

"Raleigh calls with some bullshit story. Right then I shoulda knowed. Then the fine lady there say it some tall skinny white boy in a beat-up old Corvette and hair like a bird nest sneakin' 'round over here."

"So you automatically jump to me?"

"Yeah, I did. I call Raleigh back, tell him tell whoever call him need to get they skinny ass back out here." He grinned showing me a bunch of very white teeth. "And look. Here you is."

I didn't say that didn't exactly make him Nostradamus. I said, "What do you need me for? You've been inside."

Booker nodded about fifty pounds of head. "Yeah. Yeah, I been inside. Pretty, ain't it?"

"Not so bad as a floater."

"See, now, that's why I like you, Sloan. You always got something positive to say."

Shit, I guess I had been wrong about Booker not liking me. Maybe Raleigh was wrong, too. Maybe he was the one who didn't like anybody, not Booker.

"So, what you reckon, Sloan? You gone tell me a story or I need to put you in the backseat, let you think it over?"

My last encounter with Booker wasn't entirely unsimilar. I had found a couple of stiff ones for the county and didn't feel chatty about that either. Booker and his partner Channing had given me some think time in the backseat of their car, hand-cuffed, windows up, ninety or so outside, a hundred and twenty or better in the car. About thirty minutes of that, a Gila monster would squawk. So will a Duncan Sloan.

"What if I said I need to talk to my client first?"

"I'd say maybe you need some time to think it over."

"In your car?"

"Seem to help you. I must say, it seem to help." Booker was smiling, enjoying the hell out of it.

"How about you give me an hour or so? I'll meet you some-where."

Booker put that through his large head. "You got till the ME get done. He ain't even here yet, so it'll be this evenin' sometime." I got the hard-eyed look, then, "I call, you best be available. You got that, didn't you, Sloan?"

"Yes sir, Mr. Booker, sir."

"Channing inside. You want to see him? Explain your delicate position to him?"

"No."

"Then I suggest you gimme a good phone number and then you get your ass in that black car, and you get the fuck out from in front of me before I come to my senses."

I did as suggested.

10

The East-West took me back to I-4 westbound, which actually took me south to southbound OBT. I U-turned, went north on the Trail the block and a half to the Hio. No one had patched the potholes in the parking lot while I was away.

It was nearly four, so the sun was still proud over the pink sign, but not like yesterday at two, still hot enough that if someone had asked if it was hot enough for me, I'd have said yeah.

Dodging craters, crossing the lot, through the window I could see the madam shooing Hamid to the rear. He gave her his two-handed flap and went through the back as I came in the front.

"Ahh, Mr. Sloan."

I felt like a goat at Gatorland.

"How's life treating you?"

"It is excellent. Now that you are here, everything is excellent. Let me tell you things."

"Shoot," got me a puzzled look. I replaced it with, "Go ahead."

"Okeh," as she put a card on the counter between us. "This

one, he is police." She left it on a high note, so I thought there would be more. There wasn't.

I looked at the card. A young detective named Griffs. I kind of knew who he was. Probably grunting for Booker and Channing. That meant Raleigh had to give up what he knew. "He come by today?"

"Yes. Maybe eleven, maybe twelve." Hungry eyes studied me.

"Okay." I flipped a twenty on the counter. It didn't lay there long.

Another card hit the counter. "And this one, he come after we talk yesterday. Maybe six o'clock. He also is police."

I doubted it. The card was a pretty genuine-looking ATF card with the right stuff in the right place, but with an airdale badge I'd never seen in real life, like someone's creativity had gotten the better of them. Under that was a guy's name and a Minneapolis address and phone number. I didn't buy ATF involvement, couldn't see the why on alcohol, tobacco, or firearms in the deal. The cold finger went up the ridge of my spine again. "What did this guy look like?"

"Which," like it had two long *e*'s instead of a short *i*.

I thumped the ATF job.

"Ah. This one very nice. Tall, handsome man. Maybe like you but more . . ." She was making motions at her sides.

"Fatter?"

"No. Not fat, not this one. Other one, young one, he fat. No, like you only biggerer."

"Hair?"

"Yes. Much hair. Not like you, but much."

I couldn't keep the grin in the cage. It got out and crawled onto my face. "What color?"

"Maybe darker than you. With white here." She was going around her hairline with her fingertips.

"Eyes?" I thought about it, said, "Color?"

She tried to squint it up from her memory, then shook her head. "I do not remember. Not dark. Light color. Gray, maybe blue. Maybe green."

Let's see, that left brown that the eyes were not. Maybe. I tossed another twenty on the counter, considered Pike's financial stats, tossed another. They disappeared as a team.

"Thanks. You get something else, you know the scale."

She was smiling. "Oh, I have more now. I have save the best for last."

"Yeah?"

"Yes. I call you first time to tell you this. I am worry for you. This is why I am glad you come. Two come yesterday. Just after you leave." She let it float, wanting me to go fish.

"Right behind me?"

"Yes. Mean boys. Not so old. How is it said? Higspanich?"

"Hispanic."

"Yes. They say what do I tell you. I say I tell you we have rooms, many nice rooms, all thirty-two dollars for one night. They laugh. Mean laugh. They say you not stay in this motel. They have very bad things to say about my motel. I say leave. One, he come around the counter and take my arm. Very hard. He say I talk or they make me sorry." She stopped. I guess to let me catch up.

I took a jump ahead. "And Hamid came out and showed them his shiny chrome pistola, right?"

"Yes. They move back but talk more mean talk. Talk about killing. Hamid shoot the air and they leave."

My eyes couldn't help it, they looked at the ceiling.

"There," she was pointing at a half-inch hole in the stained ceiling tiles.

I didn't think she had the language good enough to ask if they looked like boys who might cut off someone's nipples and ears and such. I didn't need to. These boys were most likely my snippers.

She grabbed the hundred I produced before it hit the counter. I gave her a straight look and said, "You and the old man watch yourselves, all right? These boys don't play. I don't think they'll be back, but if they do, tell Hamid to shoot them both graveyard dead soon as they walk in the door."

Madam Curry's throat muscles moved around some. If she were a man, her Adam's apple would have bobbled. "You are thinking these ones are this bad?"

"Yeah. I know it. They come back, it'll be personal. You tell Hamid to shoot fast and straight. No talk."

"What about police?"

"Tell them I told you to."

11

Three good-size question marks were in the car with me when I pulled out of the Hio and pushed north to the Sugar Shack, now the Sugar Shack A-Go-Go. New owners; new girls.

I doubted it. The part about the girls anyway. Less shopworn, you could have sold me on. There was nothing on the Trail north of I-4 or south of Colonial that could pass for new, including me.

It was a little early for the early birds, I guessed. I pretty much had my choice on slots. The only shade in the parking lot was an embarrassed old live oak tree, its head bowed away from the ugly purpley-mauve block building. The tree could remember an Orange Blossom Trail when girls didn't get naked for dollar bills, when the Parliament House was a place for hetero swingers, and when dope and head jobs weren't the coin of the realm. I couldn't, but I was about a hundred years younger than the oak. I parked under the tree and it didn't seem to mind.

I sat back in the seat watching a streetwalker work the southbound traffic while I grabbed one of my question marks. Who was the good-looking, nonfat, unbrown-eyed guy with graying hair and a phony ATF card? Function eight told me my cell phone was electron hungry. I found the pigtail that mated to my car cigarette lighter and fed it a little.

Three rings in a northerly direction got me the time, temperature, and a commercial message in Minneapolis. My doubts about the authenticity of the card were confirmed, but I still owned the question mark.

The second question mark could be the same as the first. My gut told me it probably was. Who did the Hatchers ring up at the Hilton last night? Money must have been an issue, otherwise Donnie Ray would still be fucking up like he had all his miserable life.

And question mark number three, almost too big to fit in the car: How the hell, if Madam Curry didn't give the snippers any info, did they beat me to Bithlo?

I thought about it, decided any one answer would evaporate the other two. That meant they were all about the same size, and I was feeling some sort of guilt over the party at lot seven. I told myself I shouldn't, but I still did.

I locked my car and walked from the shade of the sad old tree to a sad awning with a neon promise of girls, girls, live nude girls. As opposed to what? Dead nude girls? It took five bucks to get me past a guy dark complected enough to pass for swarthy. He was behind something resembling a pulpit at the door.

About the time my eyes adjusted enough to confirm my suspicions that the bouncer and I might be the only people in the joint wearing clothes, my phone chirped. I headed for the door. The bouncer said it would take another five bucks to get back in. I told him I could live with it if he could live with it. He said he could.

Six or seven rings later, outside again, I punched the phone, said, "You ready for me?"

Booker said, "No, but it's my job. Where you at?"

"Confession."

He thought that was funny and told me so. Then he said, "You need to swing on down to see me if the preacher through with you."

"When?" I knew when.

"Oh, I thought right this red-hot would be nice." He gave me a pause that smelled like sarcasm. "If that's convenient with you, Mr. Sloan."

"Really it's not." Like I had a choice.

"Too fuckin' bad. See you ten or fifteen minutes."

"Where are you?"

"The substation on Parramore. You are familiar with our little place here, ain't you?"

"See you in five."

"I sho' appreciate your cooperation. I sho' do. Don't get lost 'tween there and here."

"Yes sir, Mr. Booker, sir."

He hung up on me.

I dug out the number for the Hilton, got someone named Reggie who got me Pike.

"Duncan."

"Hey, Ike. There's a small turd in our punch bowl."

He processed that for a few seconds, said, "I guess I should be glad it's small. What is it?"

"Orange County wants me to share with them."

"About what? Exactly?" Pike was getting cagey.

"Three dead people I turned up. Crystal Johnston's immediate family."

Silence, then, "Damn." Then, "Do you have a choice?"

"Yeah, but not one that'll leave me on the street."

Pike blew some air into the mouthpiece. "Let me see if I can raise Jay Feingle. He hasn't shown yet."

"Fuck Jay. His nose is already way into my space."

More silence. I took another turn. "I don't recall it being mentioned that I was going to be working for Jay Feingle. If it had been, I would have passed."

"Personality differences?"

"No. Nothing that complex. Just plain old garden-variety authority resentment."

Pike laughed a little for me. "You're a funny man, Duncan."

"Yeah, brutal honesty's a hoot. Lenny Bruce had a whole act built on it. Too bad it killed him. Maybe I should get out of this business; follow his footsteps."

He didn't disagree. "How will this affect our campaign?"

"Nada. Could even help if the cops decide they need to barter at some point."

"Are you asking for my approval?"

"Yeah, I guess I am."

"You know the importance of discretion here. Can you do it without dropping names?"

"Maybe." A thought floated to the surface. "If I have to give them a body, I'll put Jay between you and the cops. Give him something to keep him busy."

"I defer to your judgment."

"Done. Hope I'm loose by eight. I want to see the new letter. If not, I won't be calling you from where I'll be."

"I'll be here, whenever. Just come on."

"Good enough." I broke the connect.

Cecil Channing was outside the substation with a cigar, one of those cheap numbers with the wooden mouthpiece clenched between not so white teeth. His nose looked like a road map of the county and was only slightly smaller. He had mean blue eyes that were set too close over the big nose and a mouth puckered into a perpetual statement of disgust. As usual, he had on a dingy rayon-blend guayabera, this one was once blue. Below the four-pocket shirt were a pair of gray double-knit slacks, below that, big black skids with the ripple soles.

Channing was about half Booker's weight, but I'd rather have spit on Booker than made a joke on Channing's tab. He was one mean-spirited son of a bitch and damn proud of it.

"Well, well. If it ain't Fearless Fozdick hisself. How's it hanging, asshole?"

I looked back like he was talking to someone behind me. "You addressing me, officer?"

"You see anybody else?"

There was a nappy-haired black guy with ragged clothes and shoes stepped down in the back like they were clogs behind Channing, to his left.

I pointed and said, "The mayor there."

Channing took the beady blues off me and spat on the ground, turned a little, and growled at the guy, "I told you to get your black ass off this corner. Need help?"

The guy said he didn't and shuffled in my direction. He pointed at the cigarette I was burning, said, "Hey, bread, how 'bout one o' them scraights?"

Channing put a shoe in the guy's ass. "Which part of get the fuck outta here you havin' trouble with, Stymie?"

The guy rubbed his ass where Channing had kicked him and without looking back said, "You cain't do that shit no mo', blood. Times is changed."

Then maybe not. Channing kicked the guy in the ass again but harder. You could tell this one hurt; the guy got that beat-dog look on his face and sauntered off, still rubbing his ass.

"Good to see you still got that community outreach thing working." I was kidding.

"You need a swift one in the ass your own self?" He wasn't.

"Tell you what, Channing, I eat a lot of shit sandwiches you guys serve up, but you ever put a foot on my ass, I'll rip your fucking face off and put it down your pants for you."

We traded flat stares for a bit. "Still the tough ass, huh, Sloan?"

"Never was, Channing. But, see, I don't give a shit what you got in your pocket, you put that foot on me, me and you are gonna roll around on the ground some."

He thumped the cigar butt against a bubble top, jerked a thumb, and said, "Inside, tough guy."

I walked through the door ahead of Channing and when it had hissed shut, he hit me in the kidney. It caught me off base and nearly got my breath. Out of instinct, I swung my left arm out and around as I turned on him, landing a nice one with the back of my fist on his left ear. He bent down from it and I had my right headed for the back of his neck when someone spun me around like I was Raggedy Andy.

"Whoa up here, now." It was Booker.

Channing twisted around, squared off, and threw a straight one from the shoulder. I moved my head right and he nearly hit Booker in the face with it.

Booker shoved me the other way and wrapped Channing up in his big arms. "Whoa up now, Cecil."

Channing's face was red. Maybe enough to call it vermilion. "Assaulting an officer. You saw it, Booker. The motherfucker hit me. Assaulting an officer." There was a little blood on his earlobe.

"I ain't seen shit, Cecil."

There were four uniforms in the room, all watching the klatch.

"They seen it. They seen the bastard swing on me. Frazier, you seen it."

"They ain't seen shit, either." Booker had the hard black eyes jumping from one to the next. "Ain't none o' y'all seen nothin', did you?"

No one spoke. The four cops went back to what they had been doing.

Having lost his eyewitnesses, Channing fumed at me. "I'll fix your punk ass, Sloan. You fuckin' wait. I'll fix your fuckin' punk ass for this shit." He lost it again, struggling vainly against Booker's mass. He got an arm free and it went behind him.

Booker said, "Cecil, you pull that fuckin' piece, I'm gone bounce you on your goddam head. I'll do it. I swear, I'll do it."

Channing had the pistol out and Booker was turning Channing's right side away from me. "Put it up, Cecil. I mean it. You fixin' to fuck up."

They waltzed backward to a wall, Booker pinning Channing against a white melamine board with bright writing on it, erasing what they touched.

"Aw right. Aw right. I'm okay, Booker, let me go."

"Put it up."

Channing reached behind him, said, "Okay, goddam it. Let me go."

"You gone chill out?"

"Yeah. I'm fine. Turn me loose."

Booker let him go slowly and backed off, but not much. The pistol came back out, came in my direction. I ducked off behind Booker, and Booker hit Channing on top of the head with the side of a fist.

Channing's eyes went funny and his head went a strange direction to his neck. He went down on his ass on the linoleum. I was hoping Booker had broken his fucking neck.

Channing came back from weirdsville and put the gat on Booker. Booker laughed down at him, said, "You gone bust one on me, Cecil, you best go git that sawed-off out your trunk. All you 'bout to do with that thing is make me mad." He sort of turned his head in my direction without taking his eyes off Channing, said, "Sloan, you get your ass outta here. Now."

For the second time in a day, I took Booker's advice. I left.

My back, down low on the right side, hurt like a motherfucker. I was pissed, bitched out on adrenaline, and more shaken than I had realized at the substation. Having a county cop put you on his short list wasn't a good thing, particularly if the cop was Channing. I was thinking I may have to kill the bastard to go on breathing myself, wondering how that trick was done. Seemed like capping a cop could get real complicated.

About three blocks up Parramore, that part of Orlando that doesn't really exist, according to the tourist hype, my cell chirped. It was Booker.

"Where you at?"

"Going the other direction. Where the hell you think I am?"

Booker chuckled. "You one crazy motherfucker. You know that, Sloan?"

"We talking in a social context or a clinical context?"

"We talkin' in an actual context. Goddam, I don't know when I seen Cecil so fuckin' pissed."

"Yeah, well he oughta ease up on the public some."

"Yeah. Yeah, he ought. He 'bout had it. He got his twenty-five. He need to go on up the road. Find him a place in the mountains he can be by hisself."

"If you're looking for someone to back you up on that, put me down as a yea. Think he's coming after me?"

"Oh yeah. But I'm gone do you a favor. I'm gone hand you somethin' gone keep him off your ass."

"Gee, Booker, that's damned white of you. Just today I was telling someone how you don't like me, and look, twice in one day, you make a liar outta me."

"No, you ain't no liar, Sloan. I don't care nothin' 'bout your ass. You or no other slick-dick, pain in the ass freelance. Me and Cecil been paired up a long damn time. I don't particularly like him, neither; I just don't wanta see him fuck up."

"Well, I'm deeply touched, all the same."

"Sho' you is. In the head maybe. You north or south?"

"You asking for you or for Channing?"

"Me."

"North."

"Pull in that Seven-'leven at Westmoreland. I'll see you in a minute."

The 7-Eleven didn't have anything any better than Killian's, and it gives me a headache like any of the cheap shit, but I needed something to knock the edge down a bit. I grabbed six.

I was halfway through one when the clerk, maybe a relative of Madam Curry, came out to my car and told me I could not drink alcohol beverage on the premises, please. The edge was still on me hard, and I wasn't feeling too socially conscious at the moment. I told him to go fuck himself. He threatened me with the authorities and I told him if he'd wait about a minute and a half, a big-ass county cop would be there to give me what for.

He went back in and I could see him on the phone. He made sure I could see him, probably hoping I'd just leave. I disappointed him.

Booker pulled up in the big white Crown Vicky and the guy hustled out to tattle. Booker was telling him he needed to go his ass back inside when I walked up behind him and asked him if he minded throwing the empty in the trash for me, since he was going back inside anyway.

The guy looked at me like I might be that thing that chased Sigourney Weaver around in those sci-fi dogs, but he took the bottle. Even thanked me, though I have no idea why, and disappeared inside. I got in the passenger side of Booker's car with my bag o' beer.

"It wouldn't do no good to tell you, you cain't do that in no county vehicle, would it?"

"No."

"Feelin' like the county owe you one?"

"Yeah." I twisted the cap off number two. "You want one?"

"Yeah." He took it, put it between his hams, and backed out, taking Westmoreland north across Colonial. We were up in my hood now.

He uncapped the beer, made it go away in two tilts, tossed the empty on some yuppie's chemically addicted lawn. I grinned, "You do that to make me feel better?"

"Yeah. I guess." We rode some. "No. I needed it, too. Some fucker like Channing throw down on you, you never know how it gone play out. You just never know."

"So that shit about he needed to get the shotgun was just that? Bullshit?"

"Hell yeah, Sloan." Booker looked at me like I had asked if he thought Lester Maddox was a bigot. "I seen a motherfucker hit dead in the head with a forty cal, get up, and walk home. Seen me one hit in the shoulder with a twenty-five automatic slap the ground stone-cold dead. Ain't a game I care to play."

He put the big Ford behind a building at St. Michael's Episcopal and we finished the six. Nobody was talking.

After a while, Booker belched long and loud, looked sideways at me, like he was thinking too hard. "I'm gone tell you somethin'. Not 'cause I like you. But 'cause I trust you." He held off, putting it together in his mind. "Everybody know you got a smart mouth on the one side. On the other side, everybody know you know how to sit on somethin' when you need to."

"I'm flattered the county spends so much time on me."

"Now see, there the smart side. There the side makin' Chan-

72

ning want to shoot your ass. Now the other side got you two in that federal pen." A little pause. "Ain't nobody 'round here hold that against you. Most respects you for it. Don't necessarily agree, but respects it."

Booker gave me another shot of q.t. "Everybody know you ain't got no license to be out here playin' like you do. Know you ain't got no paper on that fourteen-shot Smith you carry, quite foolishly, I might add, stuck down your britches. They also know ain't no justice in it. Know the state draggin' they feet on puttin' you back legal. Maybe they got they reasons. Maybe they just slow. I don't really give a shit."

I didn't either, but I couldn't see where saying it would help. I also know when I'm being buttered like a muffin. My head hurt, my back was hurting, and I needed to get rolling if I was going to make it down to fantasyland by eight. "So what's this shit on Channing?"

Booker put two big hands on the steering wheel and pushed, eyes dead ahead. "It go without sayin', you do anything with this 'sides keep Channing off your ass, you go on my dookey list." He glanced over at me.

I gave him a big phony grin. "And I don't want to be on Mr. Booker's dookey list, do I?"

"No you don't. You sho' don't want that."

"Deal. Put it out there." I wanted to add: for God's fucking sake, put it out there.

"Four, five years ago, me and Cecil found us a Jamo in the trunk of a Lincoln in the old Montgomery Ward's parkin' lot on Colonial. Knowed who done it. Was a guy called Uzi. He another crazy-ass Jamo work the Diamond Club herb crowd down and across the street. Vice knowed that him and the trunk monkey been feudin' over that territory so we pretty firm on it bein' this Uzi who done him.

"Me and Cecil, we go see the man, and it go kinda like it go with you today, 'cept I ain't hip then to how fast Cecil go in his pocket. Well, the man mouth up at Cecil and Cecil come at him and this Uzi slap hell outta Cecil.

"See, Uzi ain't lucky like you. Cecil go in his pocket and cap the fucker 'fore I can stop him. Now, at the time, Cecil up on investigation on one shootin' already, and he talk me into takin' our shit down the street, kinda forget Cecil drop the motherfucker. So that where it stay. To this day. Between me and Cecil." He held up.

"That's a fun story, Booker. Where's the lever?"

He thought some more, then said, "They a Baggie in the evidence cage over to Thirty-third with the pill the coroner pull outta Uzi. Come outta that thirty-eight Cecil wavin' 'round today." He held up again. "You got it?"

I nodded. "Yeah, I got it. That kinda, sorta puts you in there, too, doesn't it?"

"I ain't shakin'. Ain't nobody 'cept Cecil to say I was there one way or the other. I don't see him tellin' nobody they a eyewitness to him bustin' one on an unarmed citizen. You?"

"No." I worked it a bit, said, "Thanks, Booker."

"You know how you gone work it?"

"Yeah. What I don't know is how do I let Channing know I know before he caps me."

"Don't sweat that part. I'm gone tell him you told me. Found out some way. Told me while we was talkin' just now."

"He buy that?"

"Don't care he do or not. You know now."

I nodded at the windshield. "I guess you think I owe you?"

"No. I think we even now. We back to scratch. You don't give me somethin' on them crackers out in Bithlo, I'm gone lock your ass up for pissin' on my investigation. That simple. You got that, too?"

I did. I gave him an seriously abridged version of what I had besides Pike. The story made him grin a lot, especially the part about Manny Q snitching the batch. I'm not sure how much of it he bought, but he gave me a ride back to the 7-Eleven, which seemed like a good sign.

12

People who don't live in Orlando aren't even aware there are hotels anywhere in the county other than the south end. Why in the hell, unless you're visiting ratland, anyone would voluntarily camp down there totally baffs me. The traffic sucks, the food is canned, and face it, you're surrounded by a lot of dupes all grinning and looking up like it's time for the big rapture.

I put my car in a spot maybe two hundred miles from the front entrance of the Hilton and hiked. There was valet parking, and I knew Pike wouldn't bitch about such luxuries showing up on my expense voucher, but I'd lost a damn nice handgun that route once and didn't make the mistake anymore.

An elevator full of tourists took me to the sixth floor. Top of the world. I waded through knee-deep carpet the color the gulf used to be to room 611 and knocked. No answer. Knocked again, louder; maybe too loud.

An As-Am pulled the door open hesitantly. He looked me over good before saying, "Yes?"

I told him I was with the Church of Scientology and was looking for an escapee named Ike Pike. He closed the door on me.

In a few seconds Steve Glass opened the door with a decent grin stretching his face, crinkling his eyes. "It had to be you. Come in."

I did.

The suite was a little smaller than a city block and might have been done by Nat Poe's decorator. White, white, and then white. Red art was screwed to the walls, and it smelled like there had been an Avon convention in here recently.

Glass asked how I'd been and I shrugged.

He wiggled his jaw around and bumped near perfect teeth together a couple of times, having an uncomfortable moment. "Look, Duncan, about how I acted in Costa Rica . . ."

"Forget about it." I hadn't; I just didn't care.

"No. It was unnecessarily rude behavior. I don't accept that from other people and I won't accept it from me. I've got some reasons but no good excuses, so I'll just apologize."

"Accepted."

"Do we get to go back to scratch?"

"Back to scratch."

He put a hand out and I accepted it. "Thanks."

"Forget about it."

He gave me a Boy Scout's grin. "Let me round up the afore-mentioned escapee. The bar's right there; knock yourself out," pointed to the obvious and went out.

I went over, scoped the bar choices, tossed myself a gin Mary, popped in a celery stalk, and sunk into a white cloud that proba-bly was a chair.

My senses told me someone was approaching and I turned to see my old buddy Don. He had on the same pathetic suit he'd been wearing the first time we'd met, sans the hat. He looked funnier now without it than with.

"Don." I dragged it out affectionately.

"Mr. Sloan. Very good to see you once again." He put the dinner plate–size hand out as I stood. I passed the drink to my left and let him crush my right.

"And you. How's things?"

"Fine. Very fine."

I didn't think he'd tell me differently even if that were the case. "Listen, Don, when I leave, how about you walk me out to my car. I've got a couple of things to run by you I don't want on the table yet."

His brow got wrinkled. He didn't know how to handle it. "I do not know about this, Mr. Sloan. Maybe you should speak to Mr. Feingle in regards to these items."

"No. This is something I need to run by you. We'll put it to Ike later if need be. Right now, just me and you." I gave him a wink that I hoped was conspiratorial. I couldn't remember ever being close enough to anyone to conspire.

"I will do this."

"Thanks, Don."

Pike came in about then, saving Don from fidgeting to death. The semi-Asian guy with the Brook's Bro's hairdo was with him, checking me out with no perceivable judgment being passed. Don looked uncomfortable for a bit, then disappeared.

"Duncan. Good to see you. Right on time. I hope that's a good sign."

I shrugged.

"This is Reggie, my personal secretary." Seemed like none of the help had last names. I was hoping I wouldn't lose mine in the deal. I was fond of it.

I nodded at Reggie, who nodded at me.

Pike's curiosity pushed him. "So it went okay with the police?"

"County cops," I corrected. "Could have been better; could have been worse." My right kidney laughed at the discretion.

"We're still in business though?"

"I'm here."

"Yes. Yes, you are. Oh, Jay's flight got canceled but he should be here any minute." He looked at the watch on his wrist. "I hope."

"Yeah. Me, too." I lied and Pike grinned.

"I spoke to Jay. I sensed there was an impending confrontation. I explained your position. He's agreeable."

"That's sweet of him."

Pike pursed his lips. "I thought you and Jay were friends, from what you had said about each other. I may have been off a little." His look was expectant.

I could have said that Jay and I tolerated each other. That I thought he was a Goody Two-shoes motherfucker. That I had fired his ass for an off-color remark he had made to a Jewish client when we were at Costa Security. That he had actually cried to Pepe Costa to get his job back, and I had refused to work him after that. I said, "Jay and I weren't that close."

"I hope that doesn't present a problem." He was searching my face for clues.

I didn't help him. "Not to me. Not as long as he stays on his side of the fence."

"I think I got him straight on that."

I said, "Good," like I believed him and went in another direction. "You got another letter?"

He put a hand out flat and rocked it. He had a smile that didn't go with the cavalier motion. "Actually, a doctor's report. And a note from Crystal."

My brow went funny, then I got it. "She's preggars?"

Pike nodded while an obviously pleased expression went on his face. "Seems that way. Reggie, have you got the envelope?"

"Yes, Isaac." He opened a valise and thumbed it up, put it in Pike's direction. Pike's finger referred him to me.

A manila envelope contained two sheets. The first was a form from a doctor with the letterhead clipped off. The other, a letter written in a childish scrawl. It said, simply: "Now you believe me? I need money. Now. Send it soon."

It looked as though Crystal had run out of places to run; she had put the Bithlo address at the bottom. I felt like I'd been slapped. "When the fuck did you get this?"

Pike picked up on my alarm. "Yesterday, about noon. Why?"

I shook my head, not answering him. "Who's seen it?"

He looked at Reggie, a question in the gray eyes.

Reggie said, with a head shake under a question mark, "Me, Donna. You and Steve, of course. Thompson in security since Jay was out." His head continued to go back and forth. "Besides them, I don't know, Isaac. Maybe Don. You'd know about him." His eyes told us he was working hard on it. "I can't think of anyone else."

Pike shrugged, putting the questioning grays on me. "Why?"

I clammed, putting a fist to my mouth, blowing through it.

Pike and Reggie kept looking at me, me looking from the one to the other, but looking on through them. I blew through the fist again, put it away, said, "Goddamn. My fucking bad."

"What is it, Duncan?" Pike getting impatient.

I was looking at Pike, speaking to Reggie. "Reggie, my man, you wanta give me and Ike a minute?"

Reggie looked at Pike for confirmation, got it. He stood and said, "Call when you need me," and dismissed himself.

When he was gone, Pike said, "For God's sake, Duncan, what's going on?"

"You've got a leak like the fucking *Titanic*, man. Somebody fed that, and I mean immediately, to a couple of Hispanic boys that are into some nasty shit."

His eyes said explain it.

"Listen, I found Crystal's parents' address last night. Somebody beat me there and snuffed them. A damn nasty job of it, too."

"It couldn't have come from your end?"

"Hell no." I was nearly yelling. I was pissed. At myself.

"Calm down, Duncan. I didn't mean it as an insult. I was just thinking out loud."

"Then stop it. Stop talking to anybody about anything. Don't think. Don't talk. Don't show anybody any fucking thing else. Aw, man."

"Duncan, I'm sorry. I don't see how I could have known."

I eased off a little. "It's not your slip. It's mine. I knew it had to be in close; I didn't know it was right on fucking top of you." I put my fingertips to my temples. "And I should have. It's my job. Now I got three dead goobers on my head. Goddamn it, Sloan, you fucking dumb-ass."

It came to Pike. "So someone in my circle called the address to someone down here and they killed these people." He was saying it, not asking it, getting it right in his own mind.

"You got it."

Concern welled up in his face. "Do you think they've found the girl?"

"No. If these people, the dead ones, knew, you bet your ass they talked."

"How could you know that for sure?"

I stopped a grin that wanted to twist my mouth and gave him some deadpan. He might as well hear it. "You think you'd talk if someone cut off your facial accessories, your nipples, the head of your dick, the ends of your fingers?"

It was Pike's turn to get the reality slap. His mouth moved to say something, couldn't, so he just sat there.

"On a scale of one to serious, we're at like pancreatic cancer, Ike."

He oh-my-Godded me and put his face in his hands; he muffled out, "I can't believe this."

"Yeah, I was having the same trouble this morning."

We sat for a while, me turning scenarios and maybes over in my mind, Pike gnashing his teeth and beating his brow. I was pretty sure I had it.

When he looked up, he was white like the room. "What do we do?"

"We shut the pipeline down. Me and you. No one else." I looked hard at him. "And I mean no one. Not Steve, not Jay, not Reggie, not Don, not your old man. No one." I was counting them off on my fingers for emphasis.

Pike was nodding.

I thought a minute. "No. We keep Don in the loop. Minimal, but I need somebody from your group I can trust. I trust Don. We keep him."

He nodded again, still very white.

Glass came in, took a read on Pike, and said, "My God, Isaac, what's going on?"

"We've got big problems." Ten seconds and Pike was already slipping.

I warned him with my eyes. Glass caught it, said, "Oh great. Now what? All of a sudden, I'm not to be trusted?" His face was going toward outrage.

I bailed Pike out. "I'm cutting all of you out, Steve. Somebody's killing people and until I know who, I'm going solo. It's not Ike's call. It's mine and I stick by it."

That seemed to help. A little. "Fine." But it wasn't.

It'd have to work for now, like it or not. I pushed myself up and said, "Well, back to the mines for me."

"What about dinner? Should I call down, have it sent up?"

I made a little nauseated face, said, "I've sorta come up short on appetite after the day I've had. Thanks, but I think I'll cruise. You know, I'm a little spooked. How about you get Don to walk me down to my car?"

Glass flicked the quick brown eyes at me, suspicion flashing out. "Bullshit."

I gave him a flat stare, said, "Let me play this part, Steve. It's what I'm getting paid for." He didn't like it but he let it go.

Pike said, "Steve, will you get Don?"

Glass did what your mother hates: he yelled "Don!"

Don showed up with the plaid hat on his head, nervous as a snake at a pogo stick convention. "Yes, Mr. Steve?"

"Isaac wants you to walk Mr. Sloan out." He was looking at me though.

"Yes, sir. Are you ready, Mr. Sloan?"

"Yeah. See you people tomorrow."

Glass tossed me a curt "see ya." Pike stood, still visibly shaken, said, "Duncan, for God's sake, be careful."

I looked at him like he had told me the sea was a little salty. "Yeah."

Don and I went out and got an elevator, no talk. When it spit us out in the lobby, I asked him where the bar was. He pointed us to it and led the way.

A girl with black pants that didn't fit well and a tux shirt showed us a booth. I ordered a Newcastle to wash the gin and tomato juice away. Don ordered coffee. I held the waitress up, asked Don, "What do guys from St. Paul drink when they're drinking?"

"Boilermakers."

I told the waitress to bring my friend a boilermaker. She went away.

Don said, "I could not. I am still working."

"Don, near as I can tell, you're always working. They don't serve boilermakers in heaven. Better do one while you're still among us."

He didn't argue.

I found a bent pack of smokes in my back pocket and lit one with courtesy matches from the table. The waitress brought our order and said, "Sixteen fifty, please."

I looked at her, a little smile tugging up the corners of my mouth. "For a beer, a boilermaker, and a cup of joe?" She nodded; I shrugged. "Put it to room six eleven. And give yourself twenty percent."

She said she needed to see a room key. I told Don to show her one. He found it in an outer coat pocket and laid it on the table. The girl made a mark on the tab, smiled big and phony, and disappeared again.

I told Don about my trip to rubesville this morning while he looked at me with no more reaction than if I had been telling him what I had for dinner last Sunday.

When I finished, I said, "What's your take?"

He shrugged big sloped shoulders and told me, "This sounds like very bad business."

"Yeah." The smile was back on my face. "Any thoughts?"

"No, Mr. Sloan." This wasn't going to be easy.

Don pulled about two inches off the draft and dropped the shot glass full of whiskey in it. We watched bubbles rise.

"How about this. Who makes reservations for your party?"

He thought about it. "I would guess Ms. Donna in Mr. Isaac's office."

"You have any idea when she made them, how that's done?"

"No, Mr. Sloan. But we were to come yesterday but something arose and we were delayed. I am not privy to details of this nature."

No doubt. "Who might have been here yesterday?"

His big dumb-looking face went concentrate. "May I inquire as to why you are asking?"

I told him about the redial at the Hatchers' that got me the desk here at the Hilton.

His eyes roamed off across the room. I could almost hear his brain grinding and clanging under the plaid hat. "This, I maybe could look into. Would you like me to do this?"

"Yeah. And what about a guy named Thompson in your security outfit? What do you know about him?"

"Not so much." He paused, caution slowing him down. "You see, Mr. Sloan, there are two groups within our security division. One group, my group, are more personal security persons. Most of us are related through blood or marriage. We have been with the Pike family for quite some time."

Yeah, about a hundred years. "And that other bunch?"

He wobbled the hat around. "This group is of Mr. Feingle's making. Most are somewhat new. He has brought them in since he has headed the division. You see, we do not mingle very much. This group is into very highly technical procedures and . . ." Decency held him up.

I helped him. "They think your group's a bunch of dumbasses?"

He grinned. "Yes. This could be said."

"If it makes you feel any better, Don, I don't agree with that line of reasoning." Slow and sure not slick and snappy, that's what you need in a Don. My opinion, for what it was worth.

"Thank you, sir. That does make me feel better."

"So what's this Thompson's position?"

"He is Mr. Feingle's second."

I nodded a little. "This Ms. Donna, how about her?"

Don smiled mildly. "She is a first cousin on my mother's side."

"Okay. How about Reggie? He a cousin, too?"

That got another smile. "No. He came as a personal friend of Mr. Isaac and Mr. Steve."

"How long's he been around?"

The head factory went to work. "For several years. He is

somewhat younger than they, but I would say he has been in the company's employ for ten years or so."

"You trust him?"

"Oh, yes. He is most efficient." Four syllables assigned to the last word.

"He gay?"

Don went red, took a swallow of his 'maker. "I would rather not speak of these things, Mr. Sloan."

"It's important, Don."

"No. He is quite the ladies' man."

"Good." No obtuse triangles was a good thing. I sorta, kinda marked Reggie off the list.

"What about Steve Glass?"

The red that was retreating into Don's shirt collar rallied and attacked his face again. His head began to go back and forth. "Mr. Sloan, please understand. These are things I do not discuss. This . . . situation," he thought about it, replaced it with, "arrangement between Mr. Isaac and Mr. Steve is a very sensitive family matter. It is not to be discussed."

"Goddamn, Don, I'm not looking for a blow by blow from the bedroom. I'm asking your opinion on Steve's loyalty to Ike. His feelings on this baby deal."

"This I do not know." What he meant was: I will not say.

I let it go. No use beating a dead mule.

A high-dollar hooker was working the bar, doing a decent job of passing for coy. She was a nicely constructed redhead who had been catching my gaze when it wandered by her. She smiled at me, tilting the head down just a tad. The brazen green eyes weren't congruent with the rest of the package though. I put a dead-eyed look on her, barely shaking my head. A face full of disappointment, surprise, and disgust gave her up. She turned away and didn't waste any more time on me. No use beating a dead mule.

"How about Feingle?"

"In what respect are you inquiring?"

"What's your take on him?"

"He is very efficient." Four syllables again.

That seemed like Don's dodge on everyone. Everyone with the entire fucking organization was efficient. Somebody was way efficient.

I threw a low curve. "What's with him and Carla?"

More blush. If I didn't leave Don alone, his head might explode. "He is working with Ms. Carla at the moment on one of her Christian endeavors." I'd never heard three syllables put to Christian.

I chased the flinch. "I'm not talking business, Don. I'm talking personal. What's in that?"

"Of that, I would not be aware."

"Yes, you are."

Bluntness got me nothing. "Of that, I will not speak."

Good enough. Suspicions confirmed. "Where is Jay?"

"I do not know this. It was my understanding that he was to be here when we arrived. He was not."

"Had he been here?"

Don gave up a little in his eyes. "That, I do not know."

"Could you find out?"

"I will try. Mr. Feingle is my superior. It will not be comfortable."

"Do it. Like I said, this is all very important, Don. Important to Ike and his safety. This thing is ricocheting around right now. I'm not sure where the next bounce takes it." I thought for a minute. "Jay's hair going gray by chance?"

Don's face screwed around into a question. "No. He is very dark-haired. As he has been since I have known him."

"Help me remember what color his eyes are."

"His eye color is blue, very similar to my own. May I ask why you inquire?"

I told him about the guy passing the phony ATF card at the Hio. A light flickered in his own blue eyes, then either died or was intentionally extinguished. "These things of which you have inquired, I will do my best to accommodate."

"Please. And, Don, discretion is everything. You understand that?"

"Yes, of course. And thank you for informing me of your findings. It may help me in the performance of my employ."

"I hope. You stick to Ike like you were glued to his ass. I've worked it with Ike for you to be on my team. You alone. Fuck Jay and his boys. Got that?"

"Yes. You understand I must confirm this with Mr. Isaac?"

"Sure. And, Don, listen to me when I tell you this. I know that you're a big boy and that you put Ike's well-being way in front of your own." I gave him my most serious look. "But watch yourself. Don't go getting cute or independent. The competition here is colder than lizard shit. They'll take you down if they think you're looking at them."

"I will remember this."

I finished my brew and told Don he needed to run all this by Ike, alone, when he had a chance. We'd be talking.

Don offered to walk me out to my car. He believed I had been serious about that. I thanked him and sent him to the elevator.

The hooker turned as I was getting up, made a basically instinctive move, and showed me she'd forgotten to wear panties.

I walked by her as I was leaving and said, "I hope you're in tight with the house dick."

She gave me an unrehearsed smile, very real, and said, "What do you think?"

"I think you keep showing the monkey to the customers in here, a vice cop's gonna get some of it in the backseat of an unmarked."

She shrugged, said, "So far, there's been enough of it to go around."

I said, "I bet."

I turned to leave and she said, to my back, "How about one on the house?"

Without looking back, I said, "No such thing as a free ride, sweetheart. You and me both know it."

I could hear her laughing as I went out.

13

The clock on my dash said nine fifteen. I felt like it should be saying midnight. It had been a long fucking day, and I wanted to go home, shower, and fall in the sack. No rest for the wicked though.

Declining dinner at Pike's camp should have left me famished, but every time I thought about food, I flashed on Bithlo and lost my appetite. No grub for the wicked either, it appeared.

The Sugar Shack A-Go-Go could be on the way home if I wanted it to be. That could turn out fruitful or fruitless. If I was going that route, I'd need to hit an ATM and cash up. No dough, no know at cooch joints.

My mind free-floated around the day's events, the way it does when I'm fagged out. It floated to Natalie Poe and the hot credit card, and I got an even sicker feeling in my stomach. She was supposed to call. No, I had left a message asking her to call. She hadn't.

Blood pumped when I thought about the snippers following me to the Hio yesterday. Could they have followed me to Nat's?

My fingers went to work on her number. I got a little relief when I found my cell phone dead as a Kennedy. I remembered it had died this afternoon, and I had fed it just enough, I guess to get Booker's calls. I plugged it in and tried again.

Three rings: "Hello."

Thank you, God. I know You don't care much for me, and I don't have much use for You, but thanks anyway, big guy. "Hey."

"Hi, Sloan. Good to see you're alive. Where have you been?" I wasn't too convinced she cared.

"Working. Sorry about the cell. You try to call?"

"Yes I did."

"You get me?"

"If I did, you'd remember. Are you coming by?"

"I'm dead meat. Want to come by my place?"

I got a good piece of nothing, then, "No. I don't think so." More nothing.

"What's wrong?"

More dead cell time, then a huff, then a slice of hell. "Goddamnit, Sloan, I don't see you for nearly two months, you don't call, won't return my calls, nothing. Then you need something, you come by like you pay the rent here, push my little brother around, get what you want, and leave me smelling like a fish market the next day."

I knew she had more, but she just said, "Turn your fax machine on, if you can figure out how. I'll fax the info you wanted. Call it your stud fee, okay? 'Bye." Click.

Maybe something was wrong. I'd have to give it a month or so and call, see if she'd gotten over whatever it was she was keeping inside. I felt like a bastard.

The dark guy at the Sugar Shack said, "You back?"

"No. This is someone who just looks like me."

He didn't think it was funny. He just wanted five bucks. I obliged.

92

I showed him the picture of Crystal, and a twenty dollar bill. The way he looked at me, I might have smelled funny.

"What the fuck are you?"

"Private."

"Why do you need her?"

"She's inherited the Hughes' fortune and I need her signature on some papers."

"You think you're a funny guy, don't you?"

"Yeah."

"Why don't you take it up the street? Maybe you could find a comedy club where they could appreciate it."

"How many pictures of Jackson you need to see to tell me something?"

Never missing a lick, he said, "Two more."

I showed him two more Andys. He pointed to the door, motioned with his head. We walked out into the sodium glow of the parking lot.

"She's a popular kid, know it?"

"Yeah."

"Two spics, a midget, and now a freakin' comic." His eyebrows looked like two black caterpillars.

"Eclectic following."

His face said he needed a dictionary.

"When? The Spanish blood?"

"Two, three days back."

"The short guy was probably here today, right?"

"Uh huh. Sitting in the lot when we got here. About two."

"You know Paulie?"

He shrugged. "More like tolerate. Obnoxious little fuck."

I agreed. "Any ideas on where she could be?"

"No. No reason. How many reasons you putting up?"

"What's the current high bid?"

"Five bills."

"The small guy?"

"Yes."

"How about the Latin boys? How many they have?"

"None. Wanted to kick my ass if I didn't tell them."

"You knock their heads together for them?"

"No. I showed them what the bore of a ten-millimeter HK looks like."

I smiled. "They ever see one before?"

The man shrugged, did a move to hike his slacks up, "Maybe so; maybe no. They didn't say. Didn't have mouths in the back of their heads. You didn't say how many reasons you got to find her."

"Twice what the low boy had."

He whistled. "My, my. You've got my curiosity going. You wouldn't want to tell me why this little two-dollar trick's all the sudden worth a grand?"

"No."

He smiled for me. "I didn't think so." His eyes were appraising me. "What's it worth to put you on a bitch that knows her?"

"How well?"

"Real well."

"A C-note."

"Make it two."

I did. He wrote a name and an address on a grubby piece of paper he had found in one of his two shirt pockets. The guy surprised me with where he went next. He said, "This ain't still accurate, you come back to see me. I'll get it right."

"For two more bills?"

I got a bouncer's look from the guy. "Don't fuckin' insult me. I play it straight up."

"Sorry, friend. You never know when you're tossing bucks around."

"My business, and you're telling me something?"

I'm not big on bouncers but I almost liked him, despite his bigoted, chauvinistic mouth.

I pulled in a convenience store manned by a big Jamo and a Gandhi, grabbed a suspect meat pie and a pint of chocolate milk. Back in the car, I took two bites off the pie, flashed on Bithlo, and chucked it out the window. The milk filled the void, killed the rats in my gut.

The address was on Twenty-fifth Street. I knew the area. A street kid I used occasionally for an eyeball had a moist dump at a four-square complex on the second block off the Trail.

The area is divided into four distinct camps: low-caste white streetwalkers supporting their black-boy pimps and whatever the current addiction happens to be; crack and doojee dealers, the street corner variety, thumbnail-size bindle boys; black male hustlers who would suck a sewer pipe for eight bucks; those so undefinable by society as to be deemed redundant at best and disposable at worst. My boy Jack fit the last slot.

I pulled off the street to the sand and woodchip parking, no trouble selecting a spot. No one who lived around here had a car for very long if they ever had one. Jack's dump was through the courtyard, and I'm using that term liberally, and around a dark corner. I stuck the Smith 9 millimeter, quite foolishly as Booker had pointed out, down the front of my jeans. I wasn't expecting any shit, but in this neighborhood you'd better be ready for some.

Someone across the street yoo-hooed me. Standing on a screened porch, a high yellow who looked more like Little Richard than Little Richard does said, "You lookin' fo' sumthin', sugah?"

I had parked under a streetlight intentionally. I knew he could see me well so I threw him a set of kissy lips and turned away. He and the pussy posse on the porch tossed me back some catcalls. Lots of laughter.

Florida was about to dissolve the building where Jack hung his sneakers. The Masonite siding was gone a foot or so up, showing me some slimy, rotting framing.

Jack's about six foot six. His door, being on the outer edge of a shed roof, was about five five. The ceiling is also about five foot five at this outer wall. Jack spends a lot of time stooped over if he's home. He was.

I bumped the door twice and yelled "Jack!"

Good thing I wasn't due a piss test for anything. Jack opened the door and reefer smoke boiled out into the night like liquid velvet.

"Jackie boy."

Jack didn't speak. He backed out of the doorway to let me in. I declined, crooked a finger for him to bend and exit.

The kid doesn't say a word that isn't an absolute necessity. He wears an idiot's grin under eyes that belong to a wild creature. Fortunately, he's smarter than he looks.

When I found him a couple of years back, he was living in the woods behind Winn-Dixie at the corner of Colonial and John Young Parkway. Had been for five or six years. Nice life when living in a plywood and canvas hovel beats staying at the old man's place.

His old man was a meth freak who did crazy shit after three or four days with his eyes open. God knows what the kid had seen in his eighteen years.

When the cops evicted the ragged colony of squatters from the undeveloped land probably to pour some more concrete and call it progress, I staked Jack in his current dump. I worked him when I could to keep from having to call myself charitable. Usually, it ended up just good old-fashioned charity however. I'm going to fuck right around and have to go to heaven if I don't watch it.

"Need work?"

Jack nodded, his head bobbing rapidly five or six times.

"Know who's in the corner house now?"

His head dittoed the nod.

"Girls?"

Again the nod.

"Skinny blonde?"

The wild-thing eyes looked confused. The head went the other way.

I showed him the picture of Crystal and he gave me the idiot grin. "Hair's black, dude. Short. Black."

"Same girl, though?"

The nod and the grin.

"She still there?"

A shrug.

"Wanta check it for me?"

A nod.

Jack took off into the night; I sat on an empty cable spool outside his door.

A short stocky Hispanic kid stuck his head out of Jack's door. "Where's Jack?" He had a doob smoldering in his fingers.

"Gone."

The kid looked at the joint, sucked noisily on it, and offered it to me.

I shook my head and put a declining hand out, palm toward him. "Might push me into a psychotic episode."

The kid didn't get it, but my refusal made me suspect in his world. He stepped back in, and shut the door. He didn't have to stoop.

Ten minutes later, Jack came shuffling around a corner,

shoelaces dragging about three feet behind him. He gave me the goofy grin, said, "Gone, dude."

I did a hands-out, palms-up shrug. "For now or for good?"

He gave me back the shrug. "For good, I guess. Dude's dead in the front room." I got a grimace where the grin usually lived.

"Aw, shit. He messed up?"

A nod.

"Bad?"

Another like the other. "Dude's lost a lot of blood. Chopped up."

I rubbed my tired head with a hand and stood. I stepped on the smoke I was holding, said, "How you fixed on cheese?"

"Broke." Grinning like it was fun to be destitute.

He took the twenty I was holding out, said, "Thanks, dude."

"Sure." I used to think it was my duty to tell people I gave money to how to spend it. That's before it hit me that once you give somebody something, it's theirs and they can do with it as they damn well please. I said, "Don't smoke yourself stupid."

He put another grin up for adoption. "On a twenty?"

I shrugged, watching a rat not much bigger than a feeder pig come out of the wall, look at me and Jack like we were the ones in the wrong place, and go about his chores. "Tell you what, go down to that pay phone you own, call nine one one, tell them there's a dead guy up there."

A nod.

"You know the number?"

A grin; a nod. "Yeah. Nine one one." He thought I was jerking him.

I laughed a little on Jack's tab. "No. The house number."

A dumb look, then, "Oh. Yeah," to go with the nod.

I thought about it, gave him another twenty. "Watch your ass, kid."

No nod; no grin, just, "Yeah, dude. You, too."

I started to walk off, stopped, turned, said, "You see her again, you call me. Stay on her until I get there, it's worth a couple months' rent."

He said good-bye with one last nod, ducked, and went in his castle.

It was eleven or so when I got to my place. My message machine was blinking in the dark like mad. Throwing a finger at the machinery, a "fuck it" at the shower, and a shudder at the fridge; I hit the rack like a piece of granite. And couldn't sleep.

I got back out of bed, wandering around my close quarters in my drawers. The moon was casting a decent glow on the neglected grass of the front lawn, making the brick street look like a fallen wall. The alarm bell was clanging in my head. Had been since I'd had my chat with Don. I had thrown a wild pitch at him and he had caught it.

The question about Carla Pike and Jay Feingle had hit something. The ones about Jay had too. Not much reaction, but with a guy like Don, a blink is worth a gasp from somebody else. I knew I had a loose thread, if I could figure how to hang onto it. The problem I was having was in the area of empathy. The thread involved such a high degree of hypocrisy it escaped me.

The last thing I remember after I lay down again was a wish. I was wishing I believed in anything enough to understand how hypocrisy worked. Before I got my wish, the sandman knocked me down.

14

I woke up hungrier than a nympho's cooch, did the bacon-and-eggs thing while I rolled through the local excuse for a newspaper. A short in the local and state section, under the Other Top Stories block. A cop named Booker said three dead in Bithlo. No names till the next o' kin could be found. Good luck, Mr. Booker.

The phone rang while I was putting the greasies in the washer. I let the machine do its job. It was the cop mentioned in that other top story.

After the beep, he said, "Hey, Sloan, been down to Twenty-fifth lately? Like last night about ten-thirty?"

I picked up the receiver, got some feedback in the ear until I could unplug the machine, said, "Where on Twenty-fifth?"

Booker laughed. "I knowed you was home."

"Yeah. You psychic now? Or just psychotic?"

"Neither. I happen to be sittin' in your driveway."

I looked out, waved. He waved back. I breathed audibly. "Well, if I can't dodge you, come on in."

"That's white of you."

I had a good one about how being white was only a state of mind, but stood on it. I hung up my end and opened the door.

Booker waddled in like a duck with hip dysplasia, looking my digs over. "Damn, Sloan, I'da figured all the scratch you rake, you'd be squatin' in a decent hutch."

"My exes do. That count?"

He put out a low, phlegmatic laugh. "How many you bracin' up now?"

"Two."

"How many young'uns?"

"Two."

Booker winced and put ample lips to work on a windy whistle. "No damn wonder you always run your ragged ass 'round."

I shrugged. "That part's a joy. The ex part chaps my ass, though. You come by to plow up my marital damage?"

"No. I came by to see why come you keep findin' dead people with hunks cut out of 'em."

"The guy on Twenty-fifth? Same job?"

"You don't know?"

"No. Didn't go by myself. Sent somebody." I grinned, "Not enough fleet of foot to go cruising that cut that time of day on the hoof."

"I know what you mean. Yeah, it looks a lot like the same folks. You the one call it in?"

"No. I got the somebody else to do that, too. I had something else to do."

"Uh huh. What's that?"

"Go home and go to bed. Believe it or not, I had sort of a rough day."

I put a mug in front of Booker and a saucepan of twice-boiled milk beside it, and shoved the sugar bowl at him. He put about a half pound of sweet stuff in his coffee and smirked at the milk. I put it back on the stove.

He put the lips to work blowing and slurping for a bit, not looking at me. When he was through with that, he said, "You know I gave you a break yesterday 'cause your panties was all twisted up at Channing. Knowed they a whole hell of a lot more story than what you was giving."

"Yeah. And believe me, Booker, I was going to call the folks at Nobel and nominate your ass for the peace prize, first thing this morning."

Booker smiled. "You don't never come up short on nothin' to say, do you?"

"No."

"Uh huh. Maybe 'cept when it come to talkin' 'bout work."

I couldn't see that meriting an answer, so we sat some more.

"Sloan, you got to let me have it. You know that. Know you got to let me have it."

"That's not exactly accurate. I don't have to do anything."

"No. No you don't." When he looked at me this time, he wasn't smiling. "But either I leave here with a better story, or I leave here with your ass in the backseat of that big white car out there. You understand that, don't you?"

"I see your mouth moving, and I hear sounds coming out, but, no, I don't understand it."

"Stretch."

I finished my coffee and got up to pour myself another. "You want another shot?"

Booker scowled a little. "Shit, strong as this stuff is, I may never need no more."

I nancied my fresh dose up with the milk and some sugar and said, "I'm assuming after our little field trip yesterday, you and I have maybe moved our relationship to another level." I gave him a flat look, no expression in it.

He shrugged. "I ain't committin' to nothin' yet, but, yeah, maybe. I guess we fixin' to see."

"I lay it out there just like it is, you gonna give me shelter on my client's name?"

"Tell it and let's see."

"Not good enough, Booker, and you know it."

"You may be axin' me for somethin' I cain't deliver. Why's this client's so special. Big name? Big money?"

"Yeah. Both."

"Local?" He was trying to guess it out of me.

"No. Way unlocal. Rich Yankees."

"Mmm. Could you 'magine that? Right here in little ole Orlando. What's scarin' you 'bout it?"

"This. Somebody connected to my man is feeding a couple of Spanish boys down here." I was watching his face. He knew about the Hispanics. "You go bumping against the connection, they're gonna shut it down. We may all be shit outta luck. Forever."

Booker was nodding. "Whatchu know 'bout these Poda Rick-uns?"

"I don't know that. All I know's Hispanic. Could just as easy be Mex or Cubano. We just keep crossing paths, so far."

"That dump on the Trail. The Hio?"

"Yeah. That and a cooch joint. And I think I saw one of them yesterday. After I left Bithlo. Spanish boys over at Twenty-fifth, too?"

Booker was processing. He glanced at me over the coffee cup. "Yeah. That's what the fairies across from your boy's place say."

"My boy?"

He grinned gum deep. "Uh huh. That crazy-lookin' white boy live over in the four square." He pulled a little notebook, read, "Gilbert George Berry, aka Jack."

"He talk to you?"

"Hell no. That motherfucker move like a beam o'light. We

104

pull his ass outta the kibby smoke, got him outside, he break and run. Leave me and Channing standin' there scratchin' our balls."

"The guys across the street tell you about me?"

"Uh huh. You gone have to change cars and hairdo, you gone stay in this business."

"Maybe I'll get me a bicycle and some Groucho glasses."

"Mmm hmm. So tell me 'bout what you lookin' after for this rich Yankee."

I raised my eyebrows without putting anything else with it. "I'll give you the story. I'll give you what I've got. You want my man's name, you better take me on out to Thirty-third Street."

"Tell me the story, we'll see 'bout the ride. Where this Yankee out of?"

"Michigan."

"For real?"

"Close enough. Me and you don't know one of those cold spots from the other anyway. He's from old money. Neck deep in the military-industrial complex."

"What is that exactly?"

I grinned. "Not really sure myself. They make planes and bombs. Close enough?"

He nodded.

"The guy I'm working for is the son. He wanted a kid, so he goes to a clinic where they harvest sperm. In the meanwhile, he's running an ad at upscale universities, looking to rent a classy uterus."

"Uh huh. You tole me 'bout that yesterday. Like that word. *Harvest.* Make it sound like farming."

"Yeah. Well, a punk up there, I believe he probably came from here somewhere, the state up there gets him hooked up with a job. Work release deal."

Booker's face registered nausea. "Workin' with cum?"

My face registered amusement. "Yeah, Booker. Maybe he was a harvester."

"How they do that?"

"Hell, I don't know. Jesus, I haven't spent a lot of time dwelling on that part. It didn't seem real pertinent. You want, I'll see if I can find out for you."

"Naw. I was just curious."

"Yeah, you're that, all right. So the punk figures out who my guy is, sees he's a rich guy and his criminal mind kicks in gear. Sees money. He grabs the guy's batch."

This was tough on Booker's sensibilities; he was looking gaggy again. "Goddam. Stealin' cum." He shook his head, nearly shivering. "Why your man want his juice back? Ain't like he ain't got more, is it?"

"Fuck, Booker, just drink your coffee and listen to the story. He doesn't want the squeezings back. The punk puts the batch in his girlfriend. They start sending letters to my guy, who doesn't even know the stuff's gone. They're asking for big bucks. A hundred grand."

Booker smiled and his head started nodding. "Okay. So they gone sell the man's own kid back to him now?"

"Bingo."

"Ain't that kidnappin'?"

"I'm not a Supreme Court justice. I don't know what the fuck it is. Right now it's just plain old extortion, I guess."

"So you lookin' for the punk and the girlfriend?"

"The boyfriend is no longer among."

"Mmm. I don't suppose that's from natural causes?"

"Not unless two in the back of the head is natural."

"He get it up in Michigan? Or wherever it really is?"

"Yeah."

"But you ain't been up there?"

"No."

"Good. Good." He was thinking again. "So how you end up at the Hio?"

I balked, putting a tight clench-jawed grin on Booker. "You'll have to give me shelter on that."

"Maybe."

"It's got to do with hot plastic."

"Uh huh. The Gandhis knowed it, too. Knowed it was hot. Didn't they?"

"Probably. I told them I wasn't going to be talking about it."

"Hell, that ain't no problem. It ain't homicide. I don't give a shit 'bout no credit card."

"Good."

"So, from there, you and Raleigh work it out. The guy in Bithlo?"

"Raleigh who?"

Booker let me slide on that. "How's the guy hooked in? Daddy?"

"Step."

He was nodding. "So, you reckon the girl still livin'?"

I shrugged. "I don't believe the folks in Bithlo knew. If they did . . ." I gave him time to fit the piece in place.

"Uh huh. I get you. Maybe wouldn'ta got so nasty. Why the Spanish boys lookin' for her?"

"Got me."

"But I bet you got some ideas."

"Maybe."

"Goddammit, Sloan, just fuckin' give it to me. Quit dancin'."

I gave him another shrug. "The punk was Hispanic. Maybe they're homeboys of his. Relatives. Maybe they just want a piece of the pie. Maybe somebody doesn't want my guy to be a daddy."

"Why would that be?"

I shrugged again. If I kept it up, I was going to end up a hunchback.

"The man want a baby, why he don't go find hisself a wife. Do it the old-fashion way?"

I grinned at Booker. He was going to like this. "Maybe his boyfriend might get jealous."

I could see the lightbulb go on. "Mmm. Now I got it. Big money 'shamed 'bout his boy bein' queer."

"Come on, Booker. I don't call you a nigger; don't call my client a queer."

Booker was laughing. "You call Channing a redneck."

"Only because I can't think of anything worse to call him."

"What else you got?" Booker wanting to get back to it.

"A picture of the girl. And that's about it."

"Is that it or about it?"

"That's all you're getting."

He nodded. "You gone let me have a copy of that picture? Maybe a name?"

"Yeah, you can have a copy. The name, for what good it may do you, is Crystal Gail Johnston. By now, she knows she's in shit, I imagine. I wouldn't put too much time in on the name."

"What she do for a livin'? I mean, when she ain't extortin' money outta rich Yankee boys? Get nekkid? You hittin' titty clubs make me think she do."

"That's what I hear."

"What you gone do when you find her?"

"*If* I find her. I don't know, Booker. That's gonna be my man's call."

"Well, you keep in mind Orange County gone need to talk to her."

"Sure."

He looked at me like he maybe didn't believe me. His cop instincts were on the money. I gave him a copy of the picture and he left.

I hadn't lied too badly. That really was about all I had that was sure. To date anyway. I had the doctor who did the pregnancy testing, I had a message machine that was flashing, and I had the fax from Nat with the hits from the unmentioned credit card. It was lying on that machine when I made him his copy. I still had Ike Pike's name on my side of the table and the new black-haired, gothic look Crystal had affected.

Best of all, I wasn't sitting in a little green room down at the sheriff's department on Thirty-third. If I could keep walking around, I knew I could find this girl.

15

Natalie Poe had a point about my not returning phone calls. I didn't. Maybe she took it so personally because we had a personal relationship once.

When I'm not working, I make a point of not returning phone calls. If I'm working on an important one or I've got an ear out for an ex, I'll listen to the messages on the machine. If not, I don't know why, I just don't.

A dozen calls; two were close to pertinent.

Old news: Pike was in Orlando.

Of course Madam Curry had checked in a time or two. I was thinking I may have to give her the grand to get her to stop calling.

Nat had called a couple of times to see if I was alive. That was yesterday when she still cared.

Paulie Mopps had two. No news on one; a maybe on the second.

My boy Jack had called in a masterpiece of the succinct: "Cops, dude. 'Bye."

Booker had called to say he was coming by. That must have been right before I got up.

There were a couple more, either no talky or not worth a mention.

I got Paulie at his office. He sounded like he'd been asleep. Around a yawn he said his usual, "Paul C. Mopps."

"Whatcha got, short man?"

"The clap. Want some?"

"No."

"Hey, your girl got her hair cut."

"Yeah. And dyed it black."

He was crushed. "Oh. You heard?"

"What? You think I'm guessing? You see her?"

"No. But I talked to a girl who knows her. You interested?"

"I hope this girl didn't live on Twenty-fifth Street."

"Why's that?"

"Her boyfriend would be in the county fridge."

"Oooh. No, this one lives in Casselberry."

"I didn't think they did the skin dance in Casselberry anymore."

"Just because the prudish fucks in city hall won't let you dance naked there doesn't mean you can't live there."

"Oh. Thanks for getting me straight on that."

"Well?"

"Well, what?"

"You interested?"

"Sure."

"What's it worth?"

"How the fuck do I know, Paulie? I haven't heard anything yet I didn't know before I called you."

"Maybe you don't get nicer, you may never hear it."

"I doubt that."

Paulie laughed. "Me, too. The kid's spent the night there a time or two lately. May be back."

I puffed. "Well shit, Paulie, maybe I should call my client, tell him his troubles are over. Paul C. Mopps is on the job and might just know where the girl might be at some undefined point in the great big future."

"You're a sarcastic son of a bitch, know that, Sloan?"

"Yeah, and you're a lawyer; sue me."

"Ah, Duncan, Duncan, Duncan. You're a pathetic, twisted soul."

"Yeah? And you're a short fuck. Call me when you've got something, Paulie." I hung up.

I called Natalie, got her machine. "Nat, you there? Come on, Nat. I know you're not at work yet. Listen—"

She broke in. "What?" Not nice.

I didn't know what, so I said, "Sorry about . . ." Then I didn't know where to take it.

I got a huff, then, "Jesus, Sloan, you don't even know what to be sorry about. You're pathetic, you know that?"

"I should. Everyone I talk to tells me so."

"Only because they know you." This was going in circles.

"Well, I just called to say I was sorry."

"About what?"

"Hell, I don't know. About threatening your spoiled-assed little brother. About sacking you. About global warming. Third World hunger. I don't fucking know. What do you want me to be sorry for?"

I got a long piece of silence. "When you figure it out, maybe you can call back." She hung up.

I came within millimeters of throwing the phone through the front window. I had no more of an idea why than why I was supposed to be sorry.

The fax from Natalie was still on the machine and I jerked it off the cradle and flapped it around furiously as though that might help. It didn't.

The hits on the credit card were all over town. The doctor's charge caught my eye. His name was Partain and he had an office on the east side of town, on Goldenrod, close enough to an area called Heroin Alley to make me nervous. Other than that, we had food, clothes, a hair salon, a gun shop.

The kid did know she was in poop. She was scared. Scared enough to be toting. Maybe she was scared enough to run if she had anywhere left to run.

The phone rang. It was Pike. He didn't sound too good.

"What's up, Ike?"

"Don's been shot."

I felt like I'd been gut-punched. I got my breath back, asked a question I was afraid to ask. "He dead?"

"Close. He's unconscious."

"When?"

"Last night. We tried your cell phone, then we had to go to the hospital."

"Where?"

"In the parking lot here. Six times, Duncan. The police think it was robbery."

"Do you?"

It took a few seconds for him to say, "I don't know."

"Where was Jay while Don was getting fogged?"

"Here in my suite. He and Don had been somewhere talking. They had come back up and Jay sent him out to get some computer equipment out of Jay's car. The hotel people called up to the room. We heard the shots, but at the time, we didn't realize it was gunfire."

"Aw fuck. Where'd they send him?"

"Wait, I've got it here. Orlando Regional Medical Center. The critical care unit."

"Who's with him?"

"One of Jay's people."

"Great." I let the phone hang at my side while I thought and cursed. I could hear Pike calling my name. "Yeah, I'm here. Listen to me. Listen good. Call St. Paul. Get one of Don's cousins or something, someone he would feel good about. Get him down here ASAP. You do it; no one else. Then you and Steve, and Reggie if you want, get in your car and drive anywhere. Drive till I call you. Got that?"

"Yes. What's going on?"

"I'll call. Give me a cell number."

"I'll give you Jay's."

"I didn't hear myself say Jay should go with you."

That got me a pause. "Okay. What are you going to do?"

"I'm gonna see if I can get a cop on Don's door. If he's not dead, somebody wishes he was, and I don't know who."

"Then what?"

"I'm coming to see Jay Feingle. He and I are long overdue for a talk."

His voice dropped to a near whisper. "You don't think Jay's involved, do you?" Obviously he didn't.

"I don't know, Ike. Some fucking body is. He's as good a starting place as any. Tell him to sit his ass right there. You guys get gone."

"Okay, Duncan. Call as soon as you can." He gave me a number I could hear Reggie passing him.

I called the sheriff's department and told the lady that answered I needed Lieutenant Detective Booker posthaste. I was patched through to his car.

"Yeah. Booker here."

"Booker, Sloan."

It caught him off. "Yeah? What's up?"

"Listen, can you get somebody to ORMC like ten minutes ago?"

"Why?"

"One of my guy's people got popped at the Hilton last night."

"Mmm. Gettin' the count up, ain't you? You sure you know what you doin'?"

"Come on, Booker. The funny's gone out of it. This is a good guy. He knows who smoked him, and that who would also be the Spanish boys' contact. If I'm right."

"Uh huh. You probably right. We got people there, I'll put one on his room right this red-hot."

"Good man. Tell your deputy to run the private boy that's there off. We need this guy to live."

"What's the name?"

"Don."

Silence. "Don?" He knew there should be more.

"Goddamn, Booker, I don't know. These people aren't big on last names."

"Ain't no thang. Couldn't be many people name Don got shot out to the Hilton last night. Where you headed?"

I hung up. Maybe I didn't hear the last question.

Fifteen minutes, I was showered, in clean jeans and shirt, and booking south on I-4 westbound. I caught the East-West east to 417 south. Another twenty, I was parked on the curb in front of the Hilton. The valet asked for my keys. I broke the promise to myself, and tossed them at him. He offered to get me a stub and I asked if he'd parked many '73 Vettes today. He grinned and shook his head.

"Then you oughta be able to find it when I come back out, right?"

He said "no problem" to my back. I was going through the automatic door.

Reggie answered the door with 611 on it, taken back by my being there. Maybe it was my demeanor, or something.

"Ike and Steve gone?"

"Yes." He looked at a wristwatch. "About fifteen minutes ago."

"Where's Feingle?"

He looked at me like he wasn't going to help me. "Where the fuck is Feingle, Reggie?"

He pointed to a door across the room.

"Get lost."

"I beg your pardon." Reggie was getting edgy.

"Get the fuck off this floor."

"Mr. Sloan, I've got work to do. I've got—"

I showed him a face he probably didn't know I owned. "Then take your fancy fucking valise with you. Just get the hell off this floor. Now."

"Yes, sir." He walked past me and pulled the door shut behind him. He didn't get the valise. Maybe his work could wait.

I waded across the white carpet to the indicated door and went through it at a good clip. Jay Feingle was at a desk wearing a prissy pajama set and a stupid expression.

"Well, well. We finally meet again. How has life been treating you, Duncan?" He rose from the chair and put out a hand. His mouth was smiling, his blue eyes weren't. They were trying to read mine.

I put both hands in his chest at a full walk and took him over the edge of the desk. He rolled to the floor, said, "Hey. You hold on right there." He kept rolling, trying to get his back away from me, ending up sitting on the floor.

"Get up, motherfucker."

It was coming to him this wasn't a social call. He jumped up, going for a briefcase on the desk. I nailed him in the side of the head just above his right ear. The punch put him back on the floor, the contents of the briefcase going with him. I saw what he was after: a nubby revolver with walnut grips that bounced on the carpet.

He reached for it and I kicked him in the ribs, lifting him up and throwing him onto his back. He gagged and rolled back over to his stomach, a hand weaseling toward the piece.

I stomped the hand and put my foot on his neck. Hard. One side of his face was hiding in the carpet.

"What's wrong with you?" came out muffled by a half-mouthful of deep, luxurious pile carpeting.

"I should go ahead and break your fucking neck, Jay. How about it? Want me to break your sorry fucking neck for you?" I could see drops of spittle coming from my mouth, chasing the words. The term *rabidly pissed* would have fit nicely.

"You've already broken my hand." He had his left up, rubbing the slighted member.

I grabbed his pistol and put it in my back pocket, then got a handful of stiff, well-coifed hair. "Get up, motherfucker." I helped him.

"Ouch." He had both hands on my hand, the one in his hair.

"Hurt?"

"Yes." He had gotten around to whining.

"Good." I slapped him with my free hand, the right, across the chops. "How about that, that hurt?"

Quite wisely, he quit talking. I dragged him by the hair to the bathroom, going through his toiletry shit. I dumped his ditty bag on the vanity but didn't find what I was looking for.

We came back out and crossed the room, my left hand still full of hair. He made me happy; he went for his rod in my back pocket. I gave it to him. Across the face. He swung at me, accomplishing a wimpy punch to my back. I put the pistol on his head again. He went down against the bed.

118

Blood showed up on his brow and his head fell back, eyes freaky. The piece was laying flat in my palm. I offered it to him with a smile. "You want it?"

He shook his head, wiped a hand where the blood was, then looked at it. "You're insane."

"That remains to be seen. We'll see how you think when we're through here."

I dumped his suitcase over on the other bed, pushing stuff around with the stubby barrel of the gat. I found it. A spray can. Hair coloring. Gray. I turned and threw it at him as hard as I could. He moved his head and it caught him in the shoulder. He rubbed the shoulder, getting that rat in a bucket look on his face.

I sat in a chair and started smiling. Only with my mouth.

I put a leg on a knee, playing with his piece. Flipping the cylinder out, snapping it shut. Testing the hammer draw. Testing the trigger action with the cylinder open. My friend Jay was getting increasingly nervous.

I put my legs out in front of me, almost touching his feet with mine. I pulled a cartridge out of the cylinder and threw it at him. He never saw it coming. It hit him right between the eyes.

"Been having a good old time, huh, Jay."

"I don't know what you're talking about."

I flipped another pill at him. He missed that one, too. It hit him in the chest and rolled to his lap. He brushed it off like it was scorpion shit.

"Yeah you do." I flipped another pill. He was starting to get the hang of it; he batted that one down.

"The Pikes aren't going to like this."

"Oooh. I'm all of the sudden worried, Jay. You ever remember me being real nervous about loss of employment? I mean, not like you. Like when I fired your ass for telling old Mr. Cavanaugh how Jews were God's big mistake, and then you went in Pepe's office and cried like Tammy Faye Baker?"

119

"You're crazy, Sloan."

"Aw, come on, Jay. Make it Duncan. We're old pals here, right?" I hit him on top of the head with a cartridge. I was scaring myself; I was starting to enjoy this.

Feingle's face screwed up in anger. "I don't recall that we were ever that close."

"Yeah, me either. That's why I wondered why you gave Ike such a rousing recommendation. I felt kinda like . . ." I waved my free hand around in little circles. ". . . like somebody was greasing my ass up with KY. Know that feeling, Jay?"

I flipped the fifth pill at him. He had the game down; he actually caught that one.

"Look, Duncan, let's talk this out rationally."

"What's that?" I cupped a hand to my ear. "Is that the voice of reason, Jay?" I smiled big enough to show him my eye teeth. "Too fucking bad. No reasonable men in the room. Just crazy-assed me and miserable weaselly-ass you." I snapped the cylinder on the Colt shut and spun it.

"We're gonna talk it out, Jay. But I don't think you're gonna like the way it's gonna go." I dropped the smile. "Ready to get to it?"

Feingle had run out of words.

"Here's how we're gonna play this. I ask you something, if I like the answer, I smile and say thanks. I don't like it, I spin the cylinder on this fancy fucking handgun of yours, point it at you, drop the pin. Got it?"

"Come on, Sloan. This is crazy. I'll tell you what I know."

"No you won't, Jay. You'll tell me what you want me to hear. And, see, that's not good enough." I gave the cylinder a spin. It had a good solid feel. "So, if you feel lucky on the spin—lie to me. The odds are in your favor. What? Five outta six?"

Feingle licked his lips, his eyes on the gun.

"Wait, wait. That's not fair. You can see the cylinder, so you might know there's not one under the hammer. Tell you what, to level the playing field, I'll keep the piece behind my leg here, like this." I put the leg on the knee again, put the gun in my lap.

"Sloan, come on now. This isn't funny. You're not going to do anything this stupid."

I pulled the hammer back, lifted the revolver to Feingle's chest, dropped the hammer.

He made a little high-pitched sound and flinched.

"Now, see, Jay, that was not the truth. And I don't think this is stupid. Crazy, yeah. Stupid, no." I spun the cylinder.

"Sloan." He was back to whining.

"Okay, okay. I wanta be fair. I'll give you that one free. We'll say, like, I asked if that was you at the Hio passing the phony ATF card and you said no. So I'll ask again. Who was at the Hio playing ATF agent? Here we go, Jay. This one counts."

He looked at the leg like he had X-ray vision, then his eyes met mine. I emphasized the question with raised eyebrows.

"It was me. Okay? It was me."

I smiled and nodded. "See me smile, Jay. That's how you score. Okay, one for you; one for me. Man, this is a fun game, isn't it?"

"No."

"Aw, come on, lighten up. You get a couple up on me, you'll start enjoying it, too. Okay, let's see. When did you get to the Hilton? I mean the first time?"

Feingle searched my face, thought he found something, said, "You know when. Last night."

I took all expression off my face, shook my head a little. "Damn, Jay."

He heard the metallic click as the hammer came back. His eyes went big, his hands came up palms out, like that would help. "Two days ago."

"Good, Jay. Before you went to Miami?"

He nodded.

"You're on a roll. Now . . ." I pursed my lips and turned my eyes up. Thinking. "Who called you from Donnie Ray Hatcher's? The Hatchers or your Hispanic boys?"

Feingle was licking his lips again.

"Take your time, Jay. This one I don't know, so it's gonna be based on my opinion." I grinned big for him. "Make it good."

For a guy that hadn't been doing so good trying to read my face, he was spending a lot of time looking a me. "Both."

That got a chuckle out of me. "Damn good answer. If we don't count that first one, you may just skunk me. Why? And let's start with the Hatchers. I believe they would have been first. Am I right? Think about it. This one counts."

I got a nod and a lick of the lips. "They wanted to sell the girl."

"How'd they know where you'd be?"

Quickly: "I called and made an offer. They had to think it over."

"No doubt, they wanted to raise the ante, right?"

"Yes."

"But they said they didn't know where the girl was right then. Am I doing okay?"

"Yes. They said they could find her." Looked like we *were* on a roll.

"But you didn't believe them, did you?"

He shrugged. "I didn't know. It didn't matter much right then."

"Until your boys saw me at the Hio. Then time got slippery. So you send the freaks out there, help them along?"

"Sloan, with God as my witness, I didn't know they would kill them."

I dead-eyed him. "That's iffy, Jay."

His hands came up professing his innocence, "I swear."

"They tell you what they did out there?"

"No."

I believed him; his eyes were questioning. "You ever get the chance, you should ask." I flapped a hand. "Ah, that's not necessary. It'll come up at your trial." I gave it a beat. "Obviously they were telling you the truth about not knowing where the girl was. Trust me on that one. Okay, let's go lateral. Who are these kooks?"

"A brother and a cousin of Quesada's."

"How'd you hook up with them?"

"They contacted me."

I pulled the gat up and snapped it. Feingle made the high-pitched noise, turning his face aside. "No, Jay, that's not how that went. Let's try again and start with Manny this time."

He got his breath back, said, "Okay. When the first letter came, we got on the clinic. It was easy to tag Quesada, his record and all. Plus, he had left, no notice or anything. The timing was right. I found out from his rap sheet he was living here before he moved to St. Paul. I got his last known address down here, outside Kissimmee.

"These guys were still living at the house. All three of them were on some sort of witness relocation program from Puerto Rico."

Them and half of everybody else in Poinciana. Want a free house by Disney, a car, a chunk of money every month? Kill somebody in a heroin deal in San Juan, roll over on your compadres, you got it. The Puerto Rican government had been dumping its trash in this area for years now, lying about it. Hell, the fuckers were stumbling all over each other down there. And no one can figure why the highest heroin overdose rate in the state and possibly the highest teen overdose rate in the free world is right here in the Orlando area. Duh.

"So you generated a little interest in the Ike project and they joined up, huh?"

"I didn't really see it that way." My skeptical eyebrows got an, "Okay, okay. I needed someone down here that knew the Johnston girl."

"Cool. So you hire a couple of recycled *manteca* boys to do you a nice professional job. Got outta hand, didn't it, Jay?"

"Yes." His eyes went down. A good job of shame, but I wasn't buying it.

"Why didn't you drop them when you realized you couldn't handle them?"

"I got scared. They want big bucks now. They threatened to go to the Pikes. To keep them quiet, I have to keep feeding them money and promises."

I believed that part. "Where are they now?"

Feingle had gotten too comfortable in our little game, I guess. "I don't know."

I snapped the hammer down again. This time the squeal didn't make it out, it was just a funny sucking noise. "Where are they, Jay?"

"I've got a cell phone number. You want it?"

"Whadda you think?"

He started to rise. "I'll get it."

"You get up, I'm gonna smack your head again."

He slumped back down.

"Where is it?"

"It's written on a business card in my wallet. The number's backwards."

"My, aren't we the slippery one? They still at the house in Kissimmee?"

"I don't think so."

"You tell them to get scarce?"

He took a moment with that. "Yes. I knew you would eventually get around to it."

"I've been too busy elsewhere. So what's their asking price up to now? A quarter?"

He tried a laugh. "Half a million dollars, if they get the girl."

"Whew. You think the Pikes'll go for it?"

"Of course not. Isaac would, but he can't put his hands on that much without the old man's go-ahead."

"So you're in a hell of a spot, aren't you? Think Carla could come up with that kinda dough?"

His eye reaction was what I wanted. I could feel it coming. I was about to get another chance to scare the shit out of Jay Feingle.

"What's Carla Pike got to do with this?"

I scared him. Then I pulled the hammer back again, and stuck the heater in its place behind my leg. "Let's try that again. And come on, Jay. You're facing some tall dogs here—what's admitting you're bone dancing with Carla gonna matter? She won't get jealous, and you'll be getting all the pussy you need at Raiford. Of course it'll be stick pussy, but, hey, any port in a storm."

"You should know, bastard."

"Bold words from a man with lumps on his face and the head of his dick sticking out the flap of his fancy silk pajamas."

It wasn't true, the part about his dick sticking out, but it got what I wanted. He looked down and I leaned forward and hit him on top of the head with the gun.

"Ooouch." Whining again.

"Watch your mouth, then. So you and Ms. Carla. How long's this been going on?"

His hands were on top of his head. "Almost two years."

I tsk-tsked him. "And you two both married Christian folks."

"She's not married. She's widowed."

"Oh, my mistake. I guess that makes it okay then. You wanta

tell me how deep she is in this or are you gonna take another chance, let your chivalrous nature protect you?"

"She doesn't know anything?"

"You're sticking by that?"

"Yes." He was challenging me with his eyes.

I took the challenge. What the hell, I was the one dealing the cards. Lift and snap.

He squealed.

"Wanta try again?"

"You're not spinning the cylinder."

"Oh. Yeah, I'm not. Keeping count?" I knew he was.

"All right. She doesn't want her faggy brother to have a kid. Can you blame her? The lady's trying to get a ministry going. This kind of embarrassment could bring everything she's accomplished down in one big bang. She doesn't know any of the details though. I've made sure of that. She just wants the problem to go away. And that's what I've been trying to do."

I poohed some air and rolled my eyes. "Goddamn, Jay, it's a wonder you don't wear shining armor and ride a white horse." I grinned. "Maybe Ms. Carla thinks you do. You've showed her your lance, haven't you?"

"You're sick, Sloan."

"Yeah? I'm not the one who's got two Puerto Rican cuckoos running around fogging people. I'm sick all right. Curiosity question: What would she think about all this? If she did know the gritty?"

Feingle shrugged.

"So the ends might justify the means, huh?"

"I doubt it."

"Doubt it? Goddamn, what a couple of snakes you two are. Another one for the cat. How'd your boys get to Twenty-fifth Street? It doesn't really matter, just curious."

"I don't know anything about that."

I raised the gat.

His hands came up. "I swear, Sloan. Tell me and if I know, I'll tell you."

"You don't know anything about a pimp at a house on Twenty-fifth?"

His eyes said he didn't.

"Well, your boys are totally freelancing it now. I do believe you've created a monster, Jay."

"What is it?" If he was lying, he was fooling me.

"Oh, just some more of the same. A little mutilation; a little murder. Nothing new. Okay, let's wind this up. How did all this get started?"

"I told you. In my report. We got the extortion letter in St. Paul."

"No, no. I don't mean that part. I mean the part Ike didn't know about. The part where you told him to hire me, then had me tailed, hoping I'd put you on little Ms. Crystal?"

His mouth wanted to tell me, but his brain didn't confer.

"Come on, Jay. You've got two chances left. If you're counting. Feeling lucky?"

He couldn't do it. I knew why. His only hope in this pot of soup was a damned good criminal defense team; someone would have to come up with some major scratch. I helped him. "The old man suggested it. Didn't he?"

"You may as well shoot me, Sloan."

"That's what I figured. I'm not even gonna open that can of worms. He's too fucking old for it to make much difference. One way or the other, this will kill him in due time. Good fucking riddance."

We sat for a bit, me thinking, trying to decide how I was going to keep myself from beating Feingle to death over the next question, him licking his lips, trying to get his shifty eyes under control.

"Last round. And this gets in close and personal. See, Jay, you people all read Don as a big, stupid ox. Someone to put between the rich kids and harm's way. Just a big, dumb Polack. Barely enough sense to wipe his ass without reading the instructions on the toilet paper dispenser." I gave him a nasty pair of eyes. "I guess Ike's the only one who has any affection for the big stoop in the whole rotten bunch of you. Then there's me. See, I've liked Don from the git-go. He's not half so dumb as you people give him credit for. He's dumb all right, but in a damned sweet way. He's got more ethics in that goofy fucking hat than y'all have sum totaled. And you're gonna tell me what happened last night, or I swear," I smiled while I mimicked him, "as God is my witness, I'm gonna stomp you into this fancy fucking white carpet."

"What makes you think I had anything to do with that? The police said it was robbery. His wallet was gone. Some people saw it go down. They heard the guys tell him it was a stickup."

I was smiling again. Kind of like a crocodile. "Yeah. Yeah, I bet it looked like that. But, see, me and Don had a little chat in the bar last night. Maybe I feel a little responsible. Maybe I used him to push you a little. Maybe I'm a dumb fuck for doing it. But that was your call, Jay. Don, in his dumb, stupid way, confronted you. He knew you were here two days back. He knew you had those funny ATF cards, I bet. So maybe he wasn't so stupid as you thought. So you sloughed him off, maybe even threatened to get him fired. Although I doubt you tote the weight to do it, that's what you'd do. It would buy you time. Till today, anyway. Then he could call St. Paul, ask cousin Donna or cousin somebody to get an answer that was the truth and nail your ass." I let him catch up, though he didn't need it. He knew this part.

I told him anyway. "You're down here on this end of town, the Puerto Ricans are down here. You call them. Tell them a big goof with a plaid hat's coming out to your car. Maybe you didn't tell them to shoot him six times. Didn't have to. They took care of the shit on your shoe. How am I doing?"

"That's bullshit."

I raised his Colt, aimed it at his face.

He started blubbering, his voice gone way high. "Don't, Sloan. Oh for the love of God, don't. You'll fry for this."

I shrugged. "Maybe. I kinda doubt it. Thick walls. Lotsa time to set you up. One guy left standing. One story being told. I'd give myself fifty-fifty." I put my hard-ass face on him. "Hey, look—that's where you're at, too. Fifty-fifty. I'm pulling the trigger, Jay."

"Yes. Yes. I called them. They were supposed to . . . I don't know what they were supposed to do. I panicked."

"That's your excuse, and you're sticking by it?"

"Yes. That's the truth. Honest to God, Sloan. Please."

"Sorry, Jay. I guess I got to change the rules on you. The truth won't set you free this time. Say bye-bye."

He started saying the Lord's Prayer, his hands up in the required position, his eyes shut.

"See you, Jay." As he opened his eyes, I dropped the hammer.

It clicked on air and Jay Feingle pissed his fancy silk pajamas.

"Damn, you're a lucky son of a bitch. One more and you can have your piece back. And this is an easy one; don't fuck up on an easy one. If I been counting right, you're outta chances. What did you intend on doing with the kid when you found her? Not the crazy boys. You? We know they would sell her to the highest bidder, but you, Jay. What did you and Carla have in mind?"

His hands were still in the prayer steeple, his eyes said he'd had it. "When it started, just an abortion. That's all. Just give her the hundred thousand to get an abortion."

"Love you pro-lifers. Sounds good till it's your ass in the crack, huh? You make me fucking sick." I tossed the gat in his pissy lap. "Your turn to deal 'em, Jay. Got the balls?"

Feingle grabbed the pistol. A grin wilder than my boy Jack's came on his face. He pointed the pistol at me. "You dumb bastard. I'm going to show you what happens when you underestimate people." Both his hands were on the gun, and it was shaking like a secondhand tire. "We'll see who's got balls. Good seeing you, Sloan." He dropped the hammer. On air. And again. His eyes told me the gray stuff behind them didn't get it.

I reached in my lap and held up the cartridge I'd palmed when I was first playing with the gun. "Oh yeah, you'll need this." I gave him one last grin and a shake of the head. "Like I said, I may be crazy," I raised my eyebrows, shaking a finger at him, "but like *you* said, I'm not fucking stupid."

He fumbled around for one of the tossed cartridges beside him. His fingers were juke dancing so badly he could barely get it in the cylinder, but he did.

While I was kicking him in the face, Booker opened the door and walked in. "Sloan, Sloan, Sloan. The fuck am I gone do with you?"

16

Jay Feingle probably thought I'd been a little rough on him. That was before he found out what happens when you point a pistol at a guy like Booker.

In Jay's haste, he had not paid close attention to where he had placed that single shell in the cylinder. When he snapped it at Booker, it was one past the hammer. Booker put three in him in a pretty tight pattern around the pump. Fucked up the silk pajamas.

Bigotry can be a dangerous vice these days. And not being able to look at a guy and instantly read that he's a cop can be downright fatal. With all due respect to Jay Feingle, Booker does, at first glance, look more like a con than a cop, but, damn, his eyes are all about being a cop. I guess that I'm-a-cop-and-you're-not glare was the last thing Feingle misread in his miserable, misguided life. Too bad he wouldn't have the chance to sharpen up his reading skills. As it came down, I guess I was glad I'd had a chance to say a proper good-bye.

And it was a nice convenience for me. I wasn't sure of any of the stuff Jay had shared would go very far anyway. Even with phone records and all, it was purely circumstantial. Being dead is also purely circumstantial, but it did get him off the street and that's what I needed.

While Booker was doing his phone thing, I slipped Feingle's wallet in my pocket and suddenly had to piss. When I brought the wallet back from the bathroom, it was short one business card with a phone number written backwards on it.

Booker caught me fumbling around with the wallet and told me I needed to keep my fucking hands off stuff; matter of fact, why didn't I just get my ass out of the room. I agreed.

While I was waiting for the kid in the nice white shorts to bring my car around, the phone in the valet kiosk rang. Another kid in nice white shorts nabbed it, listened. He said, "Are you Mr. Sloan?"

I stood my ground.

"Excuse me, sir. Are you Mr. Sloan?"

I looked around like I'd just noticed him. "No."

He went back to the phone, listened some more, looked me over, nodded, then said, "Excuse me, sir. Someone would like to speak to you."

"I said I wasn't Sloan."

"Yes, sir. And I told them. He still wants to speak to you."

I put on a cheeky expression, like I thought a rich fuck at the Hilton would look when we were irritating him. "I don't have time for any bullshit. Tell the party to go to hell."

"Sir, it's a police officer."

I gave it up, grinned. "Yeah, I know." I took the offered receiver, said, "Yeah, Booker."

On the way back up, the elevator stopped at the second floor. The redheaded hooker from the bar last night got on. Our eyes met before she turned and ignored me. She looked at the keypad, saw six was lit, and proceeded to study the digital floor readout over the door.

I said, "Pull an all-nighter?" thought about it, said, "Sorry. That was uncalled for."

She raised a hand and tossed a c'est la vie over her shoulder.

The car stopped at four, doors opened on no one, closed. When it was moving again, she asked "What are you doing back?"

It was my turn to pass on making smart-ass remarks. I gave her a simple, "Business."

She turned. It was a damned shame she was an eve angel. The woman was truly beautiful. "What's your business?"

"The opposite of yours." I was getting my nerve back.

She looked amused and skeptical. "You're no hustler."

"Private dick."

The amusement bloomed, glittered in her quick green eyes. She got it. "You say it out loud, I'll slap hell out of you."

"I believe you."

"What's your name, private dick?"

"Sloan."

The doors opened on six. We stepped out on the sea foam carpet.

Her eyes did a faux appraisal, head to toe. "I *do* like to laugh. I do well, invest it right, enough to keep a suite here from time to time. You ever want to come up and give me something to smile about, do it, mon petit chou."

"What room? Six six six?"

She had a nice smile. "You've got it." She started to walk away, turned, did the head-down, eyes-up thing for me, said, "How did you make me?"

"Takes one to know one."

The lady shook the curly locks. "You're a funny guy, private dick Sloan. Come by and see me sometime. Make me laugh."

We parted on better terms than we'd started out on, me wishing my ego wasn't so goddamned enormous. I'd never gotten the nerve to roll with a pro and I wondered what she could teach me. Redheaded whores who speak French and get my bad jokes were rare and she had my curiosity going. She had something going.

Channing was in 611 when I got back. We traded insolent glares and he turned and went into Feingle's room. I guess Booker had told him I had a secret.

Booker came out, spotted me, said, "Goddam, Sloan. You worse than a teenybopper to keep an eye on. Me and you need to talk."

"About what?"

He rolled the black eyes, showing me some pink membrane in the corners. "Oh, I don't know. Why the man got knots on his head. Why he piss hisself. Why they thirty-eight bullets strowed everwhere. How you got him so jumpy he think he need to cap my ass."

"Oh, that." I dared my face to show him anything.

"Yeah, that. Where your man? I'm guessin' that ain't him." He had a thumb jerking in Feingle's direction.

"No."

"Good. Wouldn't wanta be puttin' holes in your payin' customers. Let's go someplace."

"You actually think the department's gonna let you work this?"

"Motherfucker point a loaded weapon at me? Snap it? He that stupid, he need to be dead."

I shrugged. "You wanta go get a six-pack, go behind a church somewhere, spill beans?"

Booker put the black dots on me. "I ain't real happy right now, and you pushin' it. You know it? You pushin' it hard." He grinned. "Want me to bring Cecil?"

"No."

"Then you find somewhere nice and quiet me and you can chat. Like right now."

"Yes, sir, Mr. Booker, sir."

I opened bedroom doors until I saw Reggie's valise and went in. Booker followed.

I punched up the pillows on the bed that hadn't been slept in and stretched out on it. Booker wedged himself in a big soft chair with a notebook. I'd never seen him write anything down. I guess it was getting too complicated to keep up with the cast. Maybe it was for show.

We sat for a long time, eyeing each other. Booker blinked first. "I do not appreciate you scarin' that motherfucker so bad he try and shoot me."

I rolled my eyes for effect. "Oh. It's my fault. You see me holding his hand up, pointing that Colt at you?"

"No. I seen you kickin' his head. And like I tole you, I seen piss all over him. I seen them cartridges." He eyed me some more. "I got me a good idea what went on."

"So why are you asking me?"

He shook his large head. "You a hard motherfucker to help, Sloan. You know that? You one hard motherfucker to help."

"So you're helping me? Like I'm treading water and you're handing me cinder blocks. I was doing fine until you came in, shot the fucker."

Booker tried to keep the bad-ass thing going. It finally got away from him and pupated into a grin. "Goddam, that motherfucker sho' scared, Sloan."

I grinned back. "Yeah, he was. And I can't believe we're sitting here laughing at his dead ass. The bastard's not even cool yet, and me and you laughing at him."

"Yeah, I know what you sayin'. We ought to be 'shamed of ourselves."

I grinned harder and so did Booker. Maybe it was nerves. Maybe it was that what we did to pay the rent had left us rotten on the inside.

"The hell you do to that son bitch?"

"Played a game."

"How it go?"

"It was kinda like Russian roulette. But the gun was empty."

" 'Course, he don't know that part."

"If he did, what fun would that be?"

"He talk to you some?"

"You bet your big dark ass."

"Lawd, Sloan. You a crazy motherfucker."

"That's what he kept saying." I gave him a look. "Shit, you wish you could get away with something like that."

"Yeah. Yeah, I do. Done got so civilized, we got to say 'please' and 'thank you.' 'Please, Mr. Perpetrator, won't you help me out, tell me what I need. I sho' do thank you for it.' " He grinned big. "How you make him think they a shell in the piece? That the trick."

I told him; he appreciated my ingenuity.

He shook his head. "So when he piss on hisself?"

"Last snap. I got to give him credit. He could lie, whine, and count all at the same time."

"So what you do then, you give him his gun back, him thinkin' they one left?"

"Yeah."

"He point it at you?"

"Yeah."

"Drop the hammer?"

"Yeah."

"What he look like? When he do it and they ain't no noise?"

"Like you'd look if you unzipped your pants and your dick was gone."

We both laughed pretty good on dead Jay's tab. The door opened and we put the laughs away. A uniform stuck his head in and said the ME was there and the shift commander was on his way up. Booker said okay; get lost.

When the door closed, Booker got serious. "Here what happened. You listenin'?" I nodded. "You talkin' to him 'cause you think he tied in on all this shootin' and killin' been goin' on. You and him get into it; he throw down on you. You kick him in the head a couple of times. He still got the Colt goin'. His gun. I come in, he turn and snap it off at me, I knock three holes in his ass. You got it?"

"Like a crow on a June bug."

"Good. You sit your ass tight till I tell the story a couple of times. They gone wanta hear you tell it a couple of times, too. And, Sloan, I mean stay your ass here."

"Yes, sir, Mr.—"

"And knock off that *Amos 'n' Andy* shit. I'm gettin' tired of it."

I grinned and nodded.

"And get that goddam smile off your face. This ain't suppose to be funny. Don't want no laughin' while you tellin' it. Understand?"

I did the grin and nod again.

Booker wiped the grin off his own face and went out to tell his story.

Looked like after all these years, I had fucked right around and made a friend who was a cop. Hell, nobody's perfect.

The first ring on the number Ike had given me got, "Duncan, what in the hell's going on up there?"

"Reggie call to tattle?"

"Please, Duncan, let's be a little more serious here. Yes, Reggie called. Twice. First to say you had sent him out. Then to say the police and EMTs were in our suite."

"He's telling the truth."

"What's happened?"

"Jay's been shot."

That got me a long piece of quiet. I saved Ike the tough question that was glitching him. "No, it wasn't me. A county cop named Booker."

"Is he . . . ?"

"Yes, he is."

A little more mum, then, "God. Oh God."

"Where are you guys?"

"Downstairs."

"You probably want to get another suite. This one will be off-limits for a day or two. I'll get the cops to release your stuff when I can."

"Can't you tell me anything?"

"I'd rather be looking at you when I do. Sit tight. They should cut me loose within the hour here."

"Listen, Duncan, I've been putting a lot of thought to this whole nasty affair. I'm ready to call it off."

"Too late, Ike. The die's been cast. Crystal won't walk away if we stop now. No matter. She knows who these guys are. And they've smelled blood; they're in it for the duration."

More silence. "Can't I have some idea of what happened? To Jay?"

I sighed loudly, said, "The *Reader's Digest* version goes like this: Jay and I got into it. This cop is the one working the Hatcher case. He walks in."

"Why was he there?"

"Ike, I said the short version. Just listen. He walks in; Jay thinks he's with me, I guess, points his pistol at the cop; the cop puts three in Jay. That's all I'm saying for now."

"Oh, God. I've got to call St. Paul."

"Don't!"

"Why not? I've got to let them know Jay's dead."

"Why?"

A short silence. "I don't know. I suppose I don't."

"No, you *don't*. You people need to learn to listen. This shit's pretty serious here. Starting to catch on?"

"Yes."

"Then sit tight. I'll be free in a bit. Get another room. I'll find you."

"Okay. Fine." Some quiet. "There's more, isn't there?"

"Yes, Ike. There's more. But like I said, I want to be looking at you when I tell you."

A uniform appeared at the door and crooked a finger at me.

"Gotta go, Ike. See you soon. Let it go; Jay was not your friend."

"But he wasn't the enemy either. Was he?"

"We'll see what you think after we talk. 'Bye." I cradled the phone, stretched, and walked out to cop hell.

Telling the story a couple of times was not real accurate. Try about six or seven. Same story. Over and over.

I guess it jibed with Booker's. The shift commander cut me loose forty-five minutes later. He cut the Pike party's stuff loose, too, but wanted them for a few questions later. I said fine. Talk to them about that.

Reggie was sitting cross-legged in the hall when I came out; he stood, stretching like I had. I gave him a grin. "Long morning, huh?"

"Yes, sir."

"Drop the *sir* shit, Reggie. It makes me feel old and I don't feed on respect. It makes me nervous to be patronized."

He nodded. "Okay. We've got a new suite. Six seventy. The other wing."

"Cute little redhead down that way?"

"I don't know, Mr. Sloan. I've been waiting for you, here."

"Watch out for her. She'll eat you alive."

Reggie's olive skin went ruddy, and he said, "I'll watch it." He gave me a grin, the first I'd seen out of him.

"The cops'll turn your stuff loose whenever. Get the hotel to bring it. You go in there, they'll put you on the spit."

He rolled the almond eyes. "They already had at me."

"Fun guys."

"Yes. If you're into torture."

I slapped Reggie on the back, said, "Let's go see the boss."

17

"You know Jay was sneaking around with Carla?"

"I beg your pardon?" Pike looked at me like I was naked and he'd just noticed.

"Did you know Jay Feingle was fucking your sister. Carla. Remember her?"

"You're kidding?"

"I do a lot of that, Ike, but right now I'm not."

"Okay." He wanted to smile. I know he did.

"You find that amusing?"

"No. Not amusing. More . . . ironic, I guess."

"Well, don't underestimate the modern Christian. You believe me if I tell you your old man put Jay up to this shit?"

I got the sad eyes. "Yes. That's no stretch. I'm a little skeptical about the killings though."

"Yeah, me, too. I think it got away from Jay and he was trying to ride it out. Then his nuts were caught in the machine and he got panicky. But credit where credit's due: I don't think Pops told him not to kill anyone either."

Pike put on a disgusted look. "Nice family, eh, Duncan?"

"I'm glad they're yours, not mine."

He blew some air out, an annex to the disgust. "I'm just glad it's over."

It was my turn to look funny at Pike. I even gave him a little sarcastic laugh. "Oh, it's not over. It's not even gonna slow down yet. Not till I find these Puerto Rican guys."

Pike closed his eyes, a pained looked overtook his face. "I can't believe what I've started here."

"Goddamn, Ike, you oughta convert to Islam. You'd get to walk the streets and flog yourself once a year. The fuck you trying to put this on *your* head for? As I recall, you just wanted a kid. Now it's your dad and your sister who could stand a good flogging. And if it ever comes to that, you call. I'll do the honors."

Pike and I were in one of the Hilton's several eateries. This one was called the Conch Room. I wasn't expecting any live conchs to be lurking about. Either kind. The nearest ocean was an hour or better out and I'd never seen a mollusk driving a car. The other kind, the folks from Key West, had their own troubles to pound and wouldn't be caught dead in a phony joint like this.

There were a lot of conch skeletons though, even one taller than me, looking suspiciously man-made. There were some dead palm fronds, dead crabs, stuffed fish that were probably dead, too. Maybe they should have dubbed it the Dead Sea Room. Love this fucking state.

"Are you making any progress on locating Crystal?"

"I've got people on the street." I didn't bother to say those "people" consisted of a bouncer at a titty bar, a kid who grinned like an idiot and smoked more reefer than a busload of Rastafarians, a woman in a sari who'd sell her kidneys for a hundred bucks, and a midget lawyer that considered bump and grind high art. "And a few leads to run." Uh huh. A doctor who, if running true to form for this case, was probably listed in who's who of where to get Dilaudids and bootleg quaaludes around the clock. There was a house in Poinciana where everyone would either be off to nodsville or hacking up the neighbors. If I could even find it. A backwards phone number of the loons. And, oh yeah, a place in Casselberry where Crystal was rumored to be a few days back. I was closing in all right.

Pike was nodding his head slowly, not really into our conversation.

"I'm a little curious as to why Jay would tell you all this." He put the gray eyes on me.

I pursed my lips in an attempt to chase away the grin that was finding purchase on my face.

"Should I not ask?"

"No. You shouldn't," I said.

"I suppose you feel Jay's relationship with Carla was prompting him."

"Don't be so easy on Sis. She was in it right up to her prudish little collar. You want to hear all of this?"

He thought about it. The rare anger flashed out. "Yes, I think I do. Call it self-preservation."

"You can call it what you like. You're paying for it. I'll lay it all out, if you want."

He clenched his teeth and breathed in deep, held it, let it go noisily. "Hit me."

"Okay, boss. Here it is, as told by the late Mr. Feingle. Jay was backwashing to your old man and Carla from the git-go. I don't know if you had asked for any discretion from him or not." I held up.

"I had asked. I don't think I really expected it. The letter from Quesada came and I didn't have much choice."

I shrugged. "I guess not. Anyway, and some of this I'm filling in the blanks per my guestimation, Jay follows the Quesada thing to the clinic. Finds out that the worst suspicions probably are true. Maybe. See, we still don't know for sure if Crystal's pregnant. If it's your seed or what. But the odds seem to lean that way. Your tadpoles were indeed gone.

"He does his work, locates Quesada, and then that's one I still don't know. It may have been Jay that popped him. I doubt it. He didn't strike me as having the balls to do coldblood. I'm guessing he hired it out, thinking end of story.

"His mistake. The girl runs back home. She's outta his field of play, but you've still got parenthood on the brain. Your old man tells him to get his ass in gear. Jay suggests me, figuring to play it from both ends. He's gotta have someone to watch me though." I grinned for him. "As hard as this may be to believe, I'm sorta-kinda considered a maverick in this crazy business."

I got a little smile. "Yes. I can believe that."

"He needs someone here. He gets Manny Q's old address off the rap sheet, which he conveniently forgot to send to me, I might add, and voilà he's got a couple of guys who live here and at least know Crystal. How well, I can't toss a guess at. I figure so-so. They've not found her yet, didn't know where her folks lived, but they've made some good guesses on where she might show up.

"Which brings up dead person number five: a pimp at a house that a friend of Crystal's was working out of."

"Good God, where does it stop?"

I gave him a happy face. "Where I find their sorry asses." I lost the happy and said, "And trust me, I will."

Pike gave me a look, the sad one. "You're angry about Don, aren't you?"

"Yes, I am. I'm putting that one on the personal side. How is the big guy? Any word."

He shook his head. "No improvement. He's still on the machines."

"I think he's a tough old bird. He's gonna come out the other side." I put a shrug on it. "He does, you better give him a fucking raise."

"I'll see to it. Why did Jay . . . did he? Don?"

"Yeah. We're getting there. Okay. The crazies are watching the Hio. See me. You get the letter, the last one with the address. Jay's panicking now. The boys are milking him like he's a Guernsey, so he sends them to Bithlo. He says to talk.

"They talk okay. With a pair of tin snips." I was watching Pike. That part was rough on him. Still a sheltered rich kid at heart, finding it hard to believe the real world's that fucked. "For all their work, they get nada. And Jay says he didn't know what went on out there."

"Do you think he did?"

"I'm pretty sure he and one of his boys followed me back from there. Of course, that was the next morning. You call it. Which brings up a side item. You'll be seeing a two-hundred-eighty-dollar charge for a speeding pinch I got chasing them."

He shrugged. No big deal. Maybe I should go buy a nice Armani suit, have something decent to wear while I'm following my leads. The sad part is, he probably wouldn't bitch. And I probably wouldn't know where to wear a nice Armani suit. This ain't Miami.

"Now, here's my fuckup. I run some stuff by Don. Tell him to sit on it. Make some calls; check some facts. Tell you. Did he?"

His face said no.

"I didn't think so." I shook my head. "Didn't wanta alarm you until he had it pat. Big dumb bastard."

"Duncan, Don's been my baby-sister since I was eleven years old. He was twenty-one. I'm still a kid in his eyes."

In a lot of ways, in my eyes, too. I didn't mention it though. Hell, I'm nearly Pike's age and most days I don't know what I want to do when I grow up either.

"So Jay sets Don up like a bowling pin. Calls the cuckoo company, they pop Don in the lot at the Hilton." I put my hands out, palms up. "And that's where we are. End of chapter; not end of book. Questions?"

Pike was thinking. "What did Jay and Carla have in mind? For Crystal?"

"He says a hundred-thousand-dollar abortion." His eyes flashed; the smile did, too. "Yeah. My reaction exactly. Preachin' and practicin', huh?"

A real laugh got out. "Now, that's funny."

"Yeah, maybe some pissed-off folk singer'll put it in a song."

"And my father. Did Jay actually say . . . ?"

"No. And I didn't push it. Couldn't see the point. But the way he didn't say it didn't leave much doubt."

Pike did the deep-breathing thing.

"Fuck 'em both, Ike."

"I wish I could say that. And stick by it."

"Why not. You've got Steve. You've got Don. You're gonna have a kid of your own. That's plenty of family. Fuck 'em."

"Think so, Duncan? You really think you can find this girl?"

"No doubt about it. She's not that good at staying low." I was lying, but he needed the bolster job.

"What about the Quesadas?"

I gave him a long, flat look. "Ike, I'm gonna do my goddamndest to plant those motherfuckers."

"Duncan, that's scary talk."

"Yeah, it is, isn't it?"

18

Booker and I had pretty much the same conversation an hour or
so later. Same place.

Of course, I didn't mention the part about putting the snippers
to sleep. Maybe it went without saying.

I asked him to find the Poinciana address. He said he'd take
care of that part and I could keep sneaking around behind his
back on the parts I wasn't telling him.

I bought him lunch and we parted in the Hilton parking lot. I
told him to give Channing a kiss for me. He told me I ought to
leave Channing the fuck alone. I agreed.

Thirty minutes later, I was doing some of the mentioned
sneaking around. The doctor on Goldenrod. A lie would get me
scat; I decided to try the truth. I did so rarely anymore, I wasn't
sure how it would go. I wasn't sure I even remembered how.

Dr. Edwin Partain was maybe only a couple years older than
Methuselah's father, but that didn't seem to have dulled his
razor's edge.

He didn't wear glasses, and if his teeth weren't his own, he
should have sued. The blue double knits he had on were older

than I am. So were the brown loafers. The skin on his bald head was in a close race with the shoes for most cracked and flaky. His white doc's coat looked as if he might have been moonlighting at the Waffle House as a short order cook, and I'd been in morgues that smelled better than his office. I looked around for the leeches and skull drills. Must have kept them in the alchemy lab.

"What the hell you want this girl for?" He spoke in that quick, nasal cracker twang that proved Orlando was still just two patties away from a cow town.

I was moving my mouth around, trying to read which way to go.

"Well, speak up, sonny. I ain't got all day."

You couldn't have proved it by me. The doc and I were the only ones here. "I'm a detective."

"Yeah. You told me that. You want me to think you're a policeman. Well, I don't. I don't know what the hell you are, but you ain't no lawman. Your hair's too funny lookin'. You're dressed funny. You got sneaky eyes. You look more like a dope dealer than a cop. What you want? You come in here to get me to write you a prescription for dope? You did, you come to the wrong place. I don't play them kinda games. You get that?"

Jesus Christ. I figured I'd better jump in and hang on before he got started on the Gettysburg Address. "No, sir. I don't need any dope. I just need some information."

"Information, huh? Privileged, sonny. You won't be gettin' no dope nor no information outta me. I been practicin' medicine fifty-three years come September. Ain't nobody ever walked outta here with nothin' I didn't think they needed. And you ain't gonna break that streak. You got that?"

"Goddamn, will you listen to me?"

"What? Now you gonna cuss me? Come in here off the street like you're some damned body, start cussin' me like I ain't got good sense. Why don't you get your ass outta here, huh? Go on. Get the hell outta here."

I swear if there had been a scalpel handy, I'd have just stabbed myself. Maybe that way the doc would shut the fuck up for five seconds so I could lay a decent line on him. Instead I sat, head down, trying not to give him any more ammo.

The fire died down and Dr. Partain said, "Well?"

The wayward grin crawled on my face.

"What's so damned funny?"

"I think I'm seeing myself in forty years, looking at you."

"Think so, huh?"

"Yes, sir."

"Is that a compliment? It don't exactly sound like it."

"I'll tell you in forty years."

The doc put out a high-toned laugh, like a drowning chicken. "You think I'll be around in forty?"

"Wouldn't surprise me."

The wet, fowlish laugh. "You sure you don't want no dope?"

"Yes, sir. Positive. But if I don't find this girl, she's gonna meet with some unpleasant fellows. Real soon."

"More unpleasant than you?"

"Yes, sir. Way more unpleasant than me."

That got some thinking time from the wrinkled head. "Make me believe it."

I told him about Ike, the pertinent stuff; the Hatchers; the pimp; Don; the Quesadas. He looked straight at me while I did, eyes as clear as a November night.

When I held up, he said, "Joy Marie's dead?"

"Yes, sir. A bullet to the back of the head."

"Effie Jean too, huh?" My face prompted him on. "That's Joy Marie's momma. She lived with her and that sorry bastard Joy Marie married."

"Yes, sir, then I'd say the older woman would have been her." He puckered already puckered lips, blew out a sharp note. "Goddamn, sonny. That's a hell of a note. I brought both them young 'uns into this world, Joy Marie and Crystal Gail." The clear brown eyes drifted back a few decades, hazing over some. "You know, I ain't sure I'd wanta be around in that forty you was talkin' about. The world's 'bout crazy enough now."

"Yes, sir. I'd have to agree. Will you help me?"

The eyes showed cagey. He said, "How do I know you ain't one of the bad boys?"

"I guess you don't. If I was, I'd be telling, not asking."

The off-color, mangled teeth chewed that, the eyes went clear again. "Yeah. I guess so. You got somebody to vouch for who you say you are?"

"Lieutenant Detective Booker. Orange County Sheriff's Department."

Dr. Partain put a claw up and scratched a flake loose from his scalp. It fell gently like a snowflake to rest with some brothers on his shoulder. "I'm gonna make a phone call. You sit tight."

Five minutes or so, he reappeared. "Well, you check out, I reckon. You and the lieutenant get on okay?"

I shrugged. "Okay fits."

The old laugh screeched out. "Uh-huh. He says when you leave here, you better be calling him. 'Course he put some pepper on it."

"I bet."

"He a good lawman?"

"He's honest and smarter than he appears. Yeah, he's a good cop." I could see home plate.

"Crystal Gail." He shook the antique head, bother squinting his eyes. "That child never had much chance. Her daddy got killed when she was, I reckon, five or six. Stabbed in a bar." He put the eyes on me. "Over a damned dog. You believe that? Him

150

and another drunk was arguin' over a damn pit bull dog. And that new one Joy Marie took up with wasn't nothin' but mean. Well, maybe he was sorrier than mean. What was his name, Hatcher?"

"Donnie Ray. Yeah."

"Uh huh. Piece of shit," came out under his breath. "I believe he was messin' with Crystal Gail. If I coulda proved it, I'da had his sorry ass thrown under the jailhouse." He did a slow head shake. "Her and her momma wouldn't talk about it though. But the way they wouldn't, well, it made me think so. Sorry bastard."

He came back to the present, popped the old claws together in a sharp clap. "So, what you need to know . . . ? What'd you say your name was?"

"Sloan." I was doing a head shake over a shrug. "Whatever, anything you could put on me to help me find her."

The old eyes shown like golden brown foxfire, the jaw working overtime, like he was chewing whit leather. "She's got a sister. A little older. Lives in Apopka. Peggy Lee . . . can't recall her new last name. Give me a minute. I'm not as sharp as I used to be." He was checking head files. "Crider!" You could tell he was pleased. "Peggy Lee Crider. She don't have nothin' to do with the rest of 'em though. I believe old Donnie Ray was after her, too. Sorry bastard."

"You got any idea where? Apopka's pretty big now."

The eyes flashed at me. "I'm old, damn it. I ain't dead nor stupid either one."

"Sorry, Doc."

He eased down. "Somewhere out toward the lake. Around them fern farms somewheres. Her husband's a good boy. He used to run a dozer out to the landfill on Keene Road. Know it?"

"Yes, sir. I do." Short of a prostate exam, I figured that's about all Doc Partain had that could do me good. "Doc, I appreciate it. Sorry we started so rough."

"Rough? That ain't rough. I got a thirty-four forty in my desk. It had got rough, I'da showed it to you."

I grinned for him. "I believe it. I owe you anything for the office visit?"

The eyes went hard, then cooled. "No. You find Crystal Gail. You see she gets a fair deal outta this man whose young'un she's totin'. That's all the pay I'm lookin' for."

"Deal."

"And, sonny, if them Porta Ricans is as mean as you make out, you watch your own ass. Hear me?"

"Yes, sir. I hear you. I'll be fine."

He gave me one last cack. "Yeah. I figure you will. You're a fast-lookin' gent. You gotcha a gun, don't you?"

"Yes, sir."

"A big 'un?"

"Big enough."

"You scared to use it?"

"No, sir."

"No, I don't reckon you would be. Let me know how it plays out. Hear me?"

I heard him.

I damn near dragged the exhaust system off my car climbing Mt. Trashmore out in Apopka. The lady in the weigh booth smiled when I pulled on the scale, asked if I was going to leave my car on the hill, have it buried proper. I asked for Mr. Crider. She said he went by Red and would be in a big D-9 Cat on the refuse hill to the west. He was.

Red Crider was five-seven or so. Fireplug build, fireplug red from head to all I could see. The name fit.

His pale blue eyes squinted suspiciously when I waved him

down. It didn't stop while he climbed off the Cat and walked over to me. Red was a close talker. I'm apprehensive about close talkers anyway. When they push garbage around professionally, I found they make me fight my instincts to back away. I stood my ground.

Red looked me over good, looked at my old Vette, said, "Whatcha need, partner?" He knew I wasn't looking to dump anything.

"Crystal Gail."

Some people think slow. Usually, they think good if you just wait them out. I had to wait Crider out. He kept the blues on me, wobbled a used load of Red Man out, refilled from a pouch he found in the back pocket of khaki pants. He was still in my face, close enough I could smell the sweetbread tang of the fresh chew over the landfill's oven blast.

He turned his head and spit a splash the color of used motor oil, eyes never leaving mine. Right before I took another turn, Red said, "Why?"

"She's in deep shit."

Another brown splash danced off the yellow clay then died. "Tell me somethin' new, partner. That girl's been wadin' in deep shit since I knowed 'er."

"Anybody killed her yet?"

Red Crider didn't swap expressions. "Not as I know of. Who are you, mister?"

"Private detective."

We had to hold off to think about that a while.

"Who you workin' for?"

"Red, my friend, that's a long goddamn story."

"Don't be makin' me your friend. I don't know you from Adam, partner. And, what's more, you don't look like somebody that'd be one of my friends."

"Then how about you don't make me your partner. Because I

don't take on partners. And what's more, if I did, you don't look like someone *I'd* pick."

This could have gone one of two ways. Since I wasn't doubled over from a quick one to the plex, I watched the eyes. The jaw clenched first, then the eyes flashed merriment. Head turn; spit.

"Naw. I don't reckon I do. You got a card or somethin' sayin' who you are you?"

I showed him one. You'd have thought it was a detailed instruction manual for building an electron accelerator. It had three lines: my name; CRISIS ABATEMENT; my phone number. He spent a good three minutes on it.

"Hang on."

Red Crider crawled back up the big Cat. I could see him punching my number in a phone in the cab. I could have told him I wasn't home.

Back down, back in my space, he said, "Say 'leave a message.' "

"This is Sloan. Leave a message if you think it'll do you any good."

Red Crider showed me a set of wide-spaced, worn teeth. I couldn't tell if it was a grimace or a smile. "That ain't a bad message. It's you aw right."

"Yes, Red, it is. Seen Crystal?"

"Yeah."

"When?"

"This mornin'. 'Fore I come to work."

I could feel my eyebrows rise. "Your house?"

"Yeah."

"You wouldn't want to tell me where that is, would you?"

"No. I don't want you over to my place when I'm not there."

"When will you be there?"

I saw some more tobacco juice flying through the rancid air. "When I get ready to go home."

"Think it'd be too much to ask when that might be."

"Naw. It'd be right now." He looked at my car. "You 'fraid fer me to ride in that fancy car of yours?"

I couldn't tell if he was serious or not. I hoped not, but I was afraid he was. Trust me, my car is not fancy. It's old. It's not even the same shade of black all over. "Let's go."

Red made one last trip up the side of the Cat, shut her down, and we left. He clocked out at the weigh office and climbed back in the car. I was ashamed. He didn't smell at all.

Following Red's directions, a right and two or three lefts took us to a street where wood-sided houses backed up into some decent-size pines. Red pointed me to one and I parked.

At the door, he lost the chew into a five-gallon bucket about half full of the same. I'd forgotten he was pouching it; he hadn't spit since we left work. I wondered what happened to the brown spit, then I tried to stop thinking about it.

Crider pulled an aluminum screen door open and yelled, "Peggy," as we passed in. No answer. "Peggy Lee! Where you at, girl?" Same answer. None.

Red Crider was getting nervous. He yelled louder, a bull bellow. Somewhere in the back of the house, a baby cried. Red charged; I followed.

He opened a door on a room full of baby smells. The ladder-sided crib was empty, but the crying was louder. Red went to a closet and opened the door. "Oh, my God." He bent and stood. A red-haired, red-faced infant about a year old wailed in his arms. No doubt, Red Crider's child.

Crider looked at me like I could explain. I held my expression. I was afraid I knew where Peggy Sue was. I was hoping she was alive.

The wailing baby was feeding Crider's panic. He said, "Mister, what the hell's goin' on?"

I stood pat.

Red bellowed at me, "What the hell's goin' on? Where's my wife?"

I blew out some air, said, "Why don't you feed the baby. We'll talk."

"I ain't got time for nonsense. I gotta find Peggy."

"It's not that simple, Red. Take care of the baby."

His broad, red face was stunned. His woman was gone. He didn't get it. "Where the hell's my wife?"

I was glad he was holding the baby. If not he'd have been on me. "I think I can find out. It's not good, Red." The baby was wailing like an August storm. "Give me the baby. I'll feed it." I put out my hands.

He turned away from me. "No."

"Red, you gotta chill out. For the kid's sake. Where's the bottle stuff. I'll get one going."

Defeat slammed him hard enough to knock tears from his eyes. "In the kitchen. It's premixed stuff. She's old enough you ain't got to heat it."

I headed to the kitchen, found baby juice in the fridge. When I turned, Red was in the doorway. The baby had gone quiet. I gave her the bottle. The baby's hands went to it.

He swiped at his face with a freckled hand glowing with fine amber hairs. "It's this shit Crystal's in. Ain't it?"

I nodded, lips pursed.

"You think we can find 'em?"

"Think so." I hoped so.

Red was nodding, looking at the kid. "I'll call my momma. She can take care of Shawna." He looked back at me, no tears now. "Then me and you's goin' to go find 'em."

I shook my head. "This is dirty business, Red. There's six dead and one down already. Stay with your kid."

Red Crider's face went graveyard serious. "You try and stop me."

I passed on the offer. "You gotta gun?"

"Yes, sir. Mossberg Home Defender. Can use it, too. Got two boxes o' double aught to go in it." He shifted the kid to the other hip. "Mister, you got to let me go with you. Hell's bells, I'd go slap-damn nuts sittin' here."

I closed my eyes and shook my head. "Red, man, I can't do it. I don't have time to watch my ass and your ass both."

Crider puffed like a toad. "I ain't no fuckin' pussy, Mr. Sloan." He glanced at the baby, said, "Sorry, Shawna." The baby smiled and slapped at the jowly face. "I was with the marines for eight years. Seen action in Kuwait. 'Fore that I was one of the ones brought Noriega outta Panama. I can move okay."

He wanted to paint himself as a tough guy, so I let him have it. "What if Peggy's already dead? What if you end up that way? Your daughter be okay growing up an orphan?"

The sky blue eyes misted over again. "Better'n livin' with a man who wouldn't go git her momma."

"Goddamn." I was thinking I wasn't going to get out of here without him, but I'd damn sure try. "Okay. Let me make a call or two. See what I can flush up."

Red Crider pointed me to a wall phone by the back door. I found the card I'd gotten from Feingle's wallet while Red called his mother and spoke softly for a minute or two. He handed the phone over, I punched the number in backwards, stepped out the back door.

Three rings. "Allo?"

"This Quesada?"

"Who the fuck askin'?"

"The guy that smoked Feingle." The lie got me a stall.

I could hear him talking to someone in Spanish. He came back with, "Jay Feingle no alive?"

"*Está muerto, hombre.* You wanta join him?"

A laugh. "If you no tougher than he is, you makin' jokes."

"When I start joking, I'll tell you since you're too fucking stupid to guess." I wanted him pissed. I missed.

"You want me to keel the women, asshole?"

"No. I wanta give you some money. You walk one way with it; I walk the other way with the women."

"Good. Now you talkin'. Who you?"

"I work for the man with the money."

He got it. "Okay. You the Corvette man. You that private cop. Right?"

"You got it, Einstein."

"Hey, you watch you mouth, asshole. I like to cut women. You like that?"

"You cut one of them, I put your dick in your mouth. That's a promise, *pendejo.*"

I got a nasty low laugh. "Yeah, Jay say you a bad fucker. We maybe see before this over, hey?"

"I'm looking forward to it. What's your name, *puta*?"

"You can call me Pedro. When you get some money?"

"When we decide how much. What you looking for? A couple of grand?"

Another laugh. "We tell Jay one half million. Sounds good, hey?"

I gave him back the laugh. "Come on, Pedro, you're acting like a cane cutter. You boys have no idea about money, do you? That's more than your entire family will make in their lifetimes."

"Hey, I make good money before I come here."

"Yeah, I bet. Like fifty bucks a week, all the beans and rice you can eat. Say a number that doesn't make me laugh."

Pedro dropped some more Spanish, got some back. No one

was laughing on his end. A good sign. "We think maybe two hundred thousand."

"I think maybe one hundred thousand."

More Spanish. "One fifty."

"Deal." He was boring me. "I'll get with my guy, see when he can have it."

"He need to make it soon."

"Come on, Pedro. It takes a couple of days to get bucks like that. How you want it?"

He hadn't even thought that far yet. More Spanish went around. "Small bills."

"Come on, dumb-ass. Act like you know what you're doing. You know what a hundred and a half large in small bills looks like?"

"Okay. Hundreds and five hundreds. Maybe some thousands."

"Jesus Christ. You guys just fell off the plantain truck, didn't you? Let me help you out. I'll make it twenties and hundreds. That's a decent suitcase full. You guys run with a suitcase?"

"You think you funny, hey, asshole? I am happy to cut you when we through."

"Bring lunch, fuckhead. Let me ask you, why'd you take both girls? Only one's the money thing."

"You don' ever see these girls, hey, asshole?"

"No."

"They look just the same. One blonde hair; one black hair. Both have big bellies. We don't know, so we take both. You tell me which one, okay?"

"Not a chance, Pedro. Both or none now."

The chuckle. "You maybe smart, hey? We only need one, why we have to worry about two?"

"Both or none. And I know you guys are big on cutting on people, but I want both ladies back in one piece. Got it?"

"Another fifty thousand for the pretender, okay?"

"Don't push it, Pedro. A deal's a deal. You start fucking with me like you fucked with Jay, hey, I'll walk away. I've got my money already. You want me to walk away?"

"No. I like you. I like how you do you business. You don' like no bullshit. Maybe you put none on me, hey?"

"You got it. Be seein' you." I broke the connect, thinking, Don't bet on it, Pedro.

When I stepped back in the little house, Red was sitting at a pine dinette table with a woman who had to be his mother. She put the eyes on me. A question was in them.

"They're okay for now."

Red turned, said, "You talk to them?"

"No, Red." I didn't know how to put it out there. I couldn't bring myself to be brutal with his mother sitting there. "I talked to the guys that got them."

Mom's brow went up, her dander rose. "Got them? What does that mean—got them?"

I could feel my lips pursing like they do when I'm having trouble with the truth. "Peggy's sister's mixed up with some pretty rough boys, Ms. Crider. They didn't know which one was Crystal, so they took them both." I didn't say lucky for Peggy or she'd be here dead. I said, "Apparently they look very similar." Red was nodding. "And they're both pregnant." My hands came out, palms up to perfect a shrug. "So they took them both."

Ms. Crider was looking at me like I was responsible. "Oh, my Lord. Took 'em where?"

I shrugged again. "I don't know," and threw in what could be a lie, "yet."

Red: "But you called."

"Cell phone, Red. And I'd bet it's stolen. I think I can find them, but it won't be in the next few minutes."

Twin sets of blue eyes drilled me, the mouth under Red's said, "When?"

"Tonight. Maybe tomorrow."

Red Crider hit the polyurethaned tabletop. "That ain't good enough. You hear me? That ain't good enough. What do they want? We'll give it to 'em."

I wanted to smile but that would have been cruel. "A hundred and fifty thousand dollars."

Ms. Crider repeated herself. "Oh, my Lord."

Red looked dumb.

I felt like shit.

I excused myself, said I needed to get my phone book from my car. I got in it, fired it up, and came out of the drive sideways, throwing pine chips in the street.

I jumped the stop sign where Country Rose Lane hit McCormick Road, went east, putting the tired old three hundred horses to task. I kept expecting to look back and see the two-story pickup that was in Red's yard behind me. I didn't and I was glad I didn't. Sorry, Red, this ain't no picnic in Panama.

19

The woman at the sheriff's department told me Booker was off duty. I asked if she had a home number on him. She did but I didn't get it. She told me his partner was there and I told her I'd rather put a cigarette out in my eye than talk to Channing. Obviously she knew Cecil Channing. She agreed.

The obligatory five tries and ten-minute wait got me Raleigh Lightstep at central booking. He was giving me shit when I broke in and said, "Look, Raleigh, the guys who did the craft show in Bithlo have the girl and her sister."

It held him for a bit. "Why the fuck don't you ever just call the fuckin' police? Why you call me, Sloan? I'm tryin' hard to figure that, but cain't do it."

"I did call. Booker's not in."

"Oh. Booker the only cop in Orange County now?"

"Come on, Raleigh. That bunch can't pee without stepping on each others' dicks. You should know. Last I noticed, you still got a limp." It wasn't kind. I didn't have time for kind.

"Up to now, me and you been aw right. You keep it up, it ain't gone be."

"I've gotta get that address in Poinciana. I need it now. You want me to start crying? Beg you some? Buy you a new car?"

I got a puff over the receiver. "Where you at? On the cell?"

"Yeah."

"Me or Booker one'll call you." Click.

I hadn't made the light at Ocoee-Apopka and 441 when my cell chirped. It was Booker.

"Sloan."

"Booker."

"They got the girl?"

"Yeah. And her sister."

"How they swing that?"

"Does it matter?"

"No. Not right this red-hot it don't. I'm gone want to know later though." He held up. My gut told me that wasn't cool.

"You gonna give me that Poinciana address?"

"Can't do it, Sloan."

"Okay. You going yourself?"

More drag. "Can't do that neither."

My turn to drag. "You wanta tell me why?"

"Feds."

"Aw fuck, Booker. Don't tell me that shit. Those motherfuckers want it?"

"No. They want these boys left alone. They say ain't no proof positive they involved. Hearsay, what they callin' it."

"Yeah, that's what it is. I heard Jay Feingle say it. I know it's fact."

"Sorry, Sloan."

"Sorry, Sloan? The fuck's 'sorry, Sloan,' gonna help? These ladies have been kidnapped. Last I noticed, that's sorta illegal."

"Sound like more o' what they callin' hearsay. How you know the Poda Ricuns is got 'em?"

"I heard them say."

I could hear gears meshing in his head. "How you manage that?"

"I came across their cell phone number."

"Uh-huh. Like in Feingle's room when you makin' him piss hisself?"

"Probably."

"Probably? You sneakin' again, ain't you?"

"Probably. What's it matter. Nothing but hearsay."

I could hear Booker's lips bouncing together as air came out. "You gotta let me think a minute. I'll call back in a few. 'Bye."

"Booker, come on . . ." He was gone.

The phone rang back as I pulled in my drive. "Hey."

"Listen, and you listen good. I can't go out there. Ain't even my county. The sheriff in Osceola don't care for us Orange County folks out pissin' in his yard. My ass already in a good bit o' dookey on account o' what happened at the Hilton this mornin'. And when I think about it, I kinda think about you. You'da tole me what you knowed, it might not o' happen like it did. Mr. Feingle might still be vertical 'stead o' horizontal."

"Yeah. And the two women would probably be gator food out in Polk County in the flat woods somewhere. Listen, Booker, either help me, or get the fuck outta my way. Okay?"

"Look here, ain't no need you gettin' pissy with me. You the one slippin' 'round here. Makin' remarks 'bout people cain't piss without steppin' on they dicks."

"Fuck you, Booker. I hope you sleep good tonight." I'd had enough. I dropped him. Before I got my door unlocked the cell rang again. "Yeah?"

"You gone listen to me, goddammit."

"All I wanta hear is an address down in Poinciana. You won't give it to me, I'll figure it out. It may be tomorrow and then the two ladies may be parted out, but I'll fucking find it, Booker. And you know I will." I wasn't as pissed as I was acting. I didn't have another play.

"Eight fifty-three Walnut, goddammit. Now you gone fuckin' listen?"

"Yeah." I was smiling. Booker didn't know it though.

"Don't you fuckin' go down there by yo'self. You listenin'?" I said I was. "They's five or six o' these motherfuckers. Ain't no two like yo man said. Those two was sent up here on relocation. The rest o' the posse join 'em. The Fed I talk to said near as they could tell, these motherfuckers responsible for somewhere 'round twenty headstones in Poda Rica. They thought they broke 'em up, sendin' 'em here and there, but they all back together. The Feds is layin' for 'em but they waitin' to get some bigger boys in the net 'fore they pull it in. So, see, it's a big fuckup. The Feds is wantin' hoss people. They don't wanta fuck they ride up on some titty dancer. So I can't move, Sloan. Goddam, it ain't like I don't want to. You know it ain't."

"Sorry, Booker. I respect your position. But I'm going."

"Hell, I know you is. And if I thought I could get away with it, I'd be in the car with you. Take Raleigh. He need the exercise."

"Shit. Raleigh does what Raleigh wants to. I don't think he gives a shit what happens to me or anybody."

"You a mess, you know that, Sloan. You got all this fuckin' guilt and persecution shit in your head. Raleigh like your ass. He think a lot more of you than you think he do."

"He's been fooling me then."

"That's how Raleigh work. He 'bout fucked up as you is. You ax him. He'll go with you. He'll act like he won't, but he'll go with you."

"Yeah, sure. Maybe if I buy him a new fucking Fleetwood."

"Oh, hell, yeah. He gone want money. I ain't heard 'bout you workin' free neither. What I hear, you don't move for less than five."

No secrets in a cow town. "You sure you don't want in? I could probably get you that same five."

"Love to. Love to get a crack at these crazy motherfuckers. I do, I'm on the street. I'm too old to fuck up, Sloan. Raleigh, he got hisself a twenty-two-year-old roundheel got ways like a baby child. He need the five; give it to him."

"Thanks, Booker."

"Well, don't thank me till you walkin' off from this. You watch these fuckers. They ain't dumb as you seem to think they is." He laughed a little, said, "And, Sloan, don't shoot Raleigh in the knee. He ain't got but one good one left."

"If I do, I'll shoot him in the bad one. See you, Booker."

"Yeah." He was gone.

Pike answered the phone at the Hilton. " 'Lo, Duncan."

"How's my buddy?"

"His eyes are open, but he's not too responsive. The machines are still hooked up. The doctor finally conceded to a maybe the last time I asked. Like you said, he's a tough old bird."

"I'd call that good news. Listen, we're in a tiz. I'm about to spend some of your money. That cool?"

"Sure." No hesitation. "On what?"

"For a hundred and fifty grand, I could get parts of Crystal and her sister."

You'd think after what he'd been through lately, the ease of shocking him would have abated. "What?"

"Manny Q's posse has them. We had a talk."

"They want a hundred and fifty thousand?"

"Yeah."

A little thought. "I'll need a couple of days. Will that work?"

"Save your time. And your money. If they delivered, we'd need a shop vac to pick them up." I let that filter. "I need some help. Some able-bodied men. At least one. That's going to go out at about five grand a pop."

"Jesus. I think I should just stop asking."

"Maybe so."

"You don't think we could do it with some cash to the Quesadas?"

"Think about it, Ike. These guys don't give a shit. All they want is to get someone out alone with a suitcase full of dough. Then everybody dies. The guy with the suitcase; Crystal; her sister; anyone else in the way."

"Shouldn't you call the police?"

"I did. The federal government has these guys on the endangered species list. They're off limits to the local gendarmes. Hell of a note, huh?"

"And they know what's going on?"

"Oh, sure. This isn't as important as the futile war on drugs though. What's five or six dead people when you can get headlines on a couple of pounds of smack? Justify pissing away fifty billion a year to stop maybe two, three percent of the flow? Come on, Ike, where's you patriotism?"

"You're not happy about this, are you?"

"Does it show? It's just so fucking stupid when you could legalize it, treat the addicts, control the flow. But that would stop the money and end the game. The federal government would rather beat off than get a piece of ass any day." I laughed. "Yeah, I guess it does bug me a little."

"Back up for me. How does Crystal's sister fit?"

"Crystal had run out of places to run. They found her there. The sister looks a lot like her and is pregged up, too. The girls were smart enough to keep the players guessing."

"Why?"

"Goddamn, Ike. These guys kill whoever is in the way. The sister would be someone to talk." I thought about it. "Sorry, man. This is my world, not yours." I thought some more. "Good for you." Bad for me. "Anyhow, I'm going after them, if I can find them. I've got an address. Who knows what I'll find, but I will need someone to cover my back."

There was some silence, then a brave thing happened. "I'll go. I don't know what good I'd be, but I'll go."

"Oh, no you won't. Who pays me when you get dead, huh? Ike, I believe you, and I admire hell out of you for the gesture, but with all due respect, you'd be in the way."

"You're sure?"

"Positive. Just hang loose, write checks."

The laugh was still a little nervous. "I'm glad to see you've gotten over your timidity about taking my money."

"Never had any. You weren't listening well. When you gave over the last five, I said I didn't need it yet. *Yet* being the key word. Don't despair, you'll get a bill you won't fucking believe when this is over. Win, lose, or draw."

"It'll be my pleasure."

"I believe you. So I can make promises to mercenaries, Your Highness?"

A good laugh. "Promise away."

"Done. Tomorrow."

Barter isn't my game. I'd never make it as a rug merchant. I'm not put together that way. If I have something I don't need, you can have it. If you've got something I need, tell me a price. I'll either go in my pocket or walk off. And don't bother chasing me either. If the initial price is too high, you can kiss my ass.

Raleigh Lightstep liked the barter game, so I knew I'd be at a disadvantage. That's if he was even interested. Booker seemed to think so; I didn't. If he wasn't, I was up shit creek with a handgun. If he was, he'd rape me. I didn't need sunglasses to protect me from the future. It wasn't bright either route.

Eight tries, fifteen on hold; lousy night at the Thirty-third Street lockup. "Lightstep."

"Raleigh. You busy?"

"Oh, fuck no. I was gone go use the tannin' booth they got for us in the new recreation hall. 'Course I'm busy, Sloan. Some us works for a livin'. Don't have access to the easy scratch like you privileged motherfuckers. The fuck you want now? Found some dead people you need me to call in for your shy ass?"

"You bored?"

"Naw, dog. I always got my dick I can play with."

"Wanta go play after work?"

Raleigh got suspicious. "The fuck you talkin' 'bout?"

"Some mean-asses in Poinciana."

"Uh huh. Booker ain't gone help you, huh?"

"Can't. His uncle won't let him."

"Sam?"

"Yeah."

"Now you want me to go. Hold your hand."

"Yeah."

"Why I wanta do that?"

"Fight injustice, Raleigh. Win one for the home team. All that shit."

"Fuck the home team."

"How about five grand then." There I went, putting the whole fucking enchilada on the table. Get ready, Sloan. Hold on to you belt buckle.

"Aw right."

My turn for a q.t. period. "Excuse me. Did you say all right?"

"Yeah. Your hearin' fucked up?"

"No. My mind's going. I keep thinking you said you'd go to Poinciana with me."

"You said five Gs, right?"

"Yes I did."

"Then, I said aw right."

170

"Raleigh, I'm moved."

"Uh huh. Then move your ass to the checkbook. Make a five, three zeros, a dot, then two more zeros. When you got it done, meet me at the house. We gone need some toys."

"When?"

"Soon as you get there."

"You taking off work?"

"Dog, for five grand, I'm on vacation next break. See ya." He was gone.

20

Raleigh's digs are a condo off Rio Grande on the south side.
Decent place, mixed crowd. I was there in fifteen minutes.

I had grabbed an old black trench coat that I'd not worn in a
couple of years, knocked the dust off where the hanger bossed
the shoulders up. I changed shells in my 9 millimeter since what
was in it had been in it for a month or better. I didn't want any oil
fouling to fuck up my day. Put four extra clips in my pockets and
an old long-bill Penn Reel hat on my head. I don't know why I
grabbed the hat. It just seemed to go with the outfit.

Raleigh opened his door, said, "Who you supposed to be?
Daffy fuckin' Duck?"

I lost the hat.

Raleigh spun open a safe that was in his spare bedroom. It
looked like an Israeli wish list.

"Goddamn, Raleigh. You planning on a war?"

He put the muddy eyes on me. "I ain't plannin' nothin'. I'm
just ready."

"Where'd you get this shit?"

"A piece here; a piece there."

"Sheriff's department issue?"

"Most is."

"That AK full auto?"

" 'Course it is."

"What are those deals?"

"Flash bombs. Concussion grenades. Tear gas. Them's real grenades there."

I was shaking my head. "What happens if there's a fire in here?"

"They a fire, my ass is out the house. Here." He was handing me the AK-47.

"I'm not toting that fucking thing."

Raleigh scowled. "What? You gone use that pocket piece?"

"I know how it works. I'm fine, thanks."

"Here." Now he was poking body armor at me.

"Shit, Raleigh. We don't even know if they're down there. It's just somewhere to start."

I got a big, dark finger in my face. "This ain't necessarily 'bout you, Sloan. I don't want your ass gettin' popped and leavin' me to do the clean-up."

I took the Kevlar vest. I wouldn't touch the Russian auto.

"Where my money?"

I dug it out of a pocket. Raleigh looked at the check. I guess it passed muster. He stuck it in a metal box in the safe.

Raleigh had on a fatigue jacket over his body armor. He began putting this and that in the plentiful pockets. I was grinning.

"You see somethin' funny?"

I shook my head, keeping the grin. "No. Just didn't know you were such a Boy Scout."

"You ain't never run in a house full o' junkies, has you?"

"No, Raleigh."

"Uh huh. I 'spect this'll be your last, too."

"I can only hope. You ready, General MacArthur?"

It takes forty-five minutes or better to get to Poinciana from Raleigh's end of town. I got tutored and chastised for that long. Mostly about being serious. Got told that this wasn't a picnic, a walk in the park, a joke, no Mudd Club or CBGB's. This ain't no foolin' around.

It was nearly ten when we found the house on Walnut. There was a vacant lot behind and I parked one street over. Lights were on and we could see at least one person moving around. Raleigh had binoculars. Big surprise.

He wanted to go dead in; I wanted to do a little peeping. We compromised. I'd peep, then we'd go in the flimsy lauan back door.

I eased up through the backyard, the dog next door raising immortal hell. No lights over there though. Someone came to the back window and looked out. I ducked off to the side away from the dog.

The shadow in the window went away, someone cursed the neighbor's dog in Spanish, and a TV came up, throwing jumpy silhouettes across the side yard.

I moved back across the field to Raleigh. He was working the binocs. "What you got?"

"I didn't see but one guy. No lights in the bedrooms. You ready, Rommel?"

Raleigh gave me a look and one last sermon. "You look here— I been shot by one man supposed to be on my team. Don't you fuck up, dog. You got it?"

"Yeah, Raleigh. I'll do my damnedest not to shoot you. I promised Booker if I do, I'll shoot you in the bad knee. Okay?"

"You ain't funny as you think you is. You ready?"

I lost the funny, leaned back against the car, breathed deep, pulled the slide on the Smith, and threw the safety off. "Go."

We did. Across the open ground, by the barking dog, straight to the door. Raleigh went through it like it was a homecoming banner.

The guy sitting across the dining room in a recliner froze, his head turned to us, mouth and eyes wide as possible. He jumped up, hands between him and Raleigh and started popping off Spanish.

Raleigh crossed the dining room like he had the field, pushing the cheap dinette set aside, straight to the guy, and slammed the stock of the Kalashnikov against his jaw. The guy went down.

I cut through the kitchen to a stubby hall, hit what the blueprints would call bedroom one: empty. Bedroom two: a guy on the bed. He jumped up sleepy and disoriented, grabbed a rifle leaning against the wall. I put the Smith on his head. He lost the rifle but stood his ground so I did it again. He went back on the bed with a long string of Spanish. All I caught was *"Por favor."* His hands went up in the universal sign for please don't cap my ass. I didn't.

I snatched the ratty pillowcase off a pillow, made him stand, and put him in it, all that would go, and marched him out to the living room.

Raleigh's guy was doing about as much moving as yesterday's fish. Raleigh was pulling down shades, closing blinds. He said, "Whatcha got, Sloan?"

"A little short motherfucker." I pushed the guy in the recliner.

The guy started chattering in his mother tongue through the pillowcase and Raleigh tapped his head with the flash suppressor on his gat and said, "Shut the fuck up." The guy understood.

Raleigh kept moving, slow, a lot like a big cat. He worked his way back through the little cinder-block house a door at a time. When he had checked every nook, every cranny, under every bed, the shower curtain, he went out to the carport. He stepped back in, looked around, and took a key off a Mother Mary with little hooks stuck in her. I could hear the utility room door open, heard him say something to himself.

A paper bag was in his hand when he came back in. He had the bland expression he affects where most would be smiling.

"What's that?"

"Oh, 'bout a quarter to a half pound of smack. Packaged and ready for the street."

"Good stuff?"

Raleigh shrugged. "I don't call none of it good, dog."

I grinned for him. "Whatcha gonna do? Save it for Christmas presents?"

"Uh uh. I got me a idea though, we finish with Heckle and Jeckle here."

I clenched my teeth and breathed deep. "Ready to get to it?"

"Yeah. You got any thoughts?"

"Yeah." I was going toward the kitchen. I put a stopper in the sink and turned on both taps. When the water level was about three inches from the top, I shut them down. "We got anything to do his hands with?"

Raleigh went in a pocket on the fatigue jacket and came out with a heavy pull tie. Sweat had beaded on his forehead, trickled down his temple.

The sweat reminded me how hot I was, how wet my hairline was. "This fucking vest's hot as hell."

"Yeah. Almost as uncomfortable as bein' shot. I'd keep it on. No tellin' when we may have company. You think so?"

"No. I think the rest of the wild bunch has moved out. These guys are flunkies. Mules. House sitters."

"Could be. That don't mean ain't nobody comin' back. You wanta work this guy; I'll eyeball?"

"Yeah." I took the tie, tapped the pillowcase. *"Como te llamas?"*

I don't know if the guy could see through the pillowcase, but he looked up at me. "Paco."

"Okay, Paco, get up."

The pillowcase went back and forth. *"No hablo mucho ingles."*

"Yeah, well, me *no hablo mucho español.* Let's try this." I put my heater against his head. "Get the fuck up, Paco." His *ingles* was getting better. He stood.

"Bueno, Paco, muy bueno. Hands back here."

His English was holding. He obliged and I zipped his hands together.

"Me amarraste demasiado apretado."

"Nah, it's just fine. *Muy bueno."*

"No. Me amarraste demasiado apretado."

I tapped him on the pillowcase with a gun barrel. *"No. Es muy bueno. Sí?"*

"Sí."

"Raleigh, your boy's stirring around a bit. You wanta hog-tie him?"

Raleigh had put a chair at the front window. He looked back at the guy on the floor. The guy was kicking a leg a bit. He mumbled and rolled to his stomach. Raleigh came over, put a foot in the guy's back, tied his hands and feet. Then he pulled the feet up, tied them to the hands. I thought about Bithlo.

Raleigh went back to his perch at the window, turned, said, "Why don't you get movin', dog?"

"Yes, sir," to Raleigh. I pulled the pillowcase off Paco's head.

He was broad faced, not much black. More *indio* I guess. Freckles spilled across his nose under concerned eyes. "You are going to kill me?" A piece of hair had flipped down from its fellows like a greasy cable.

I grinned for him. "I'd love to, but no. Not unless you want me to."

"No. I no want to die."

"Good, we're making progress." I lost him. *"Bueno,* Paco. *Donde está* Pedro?"

I guess Pedro was a bad motherfucker. Paco's eyes went wild, his head went back and forth. "I don' know where is Pedro."

"Oh, I think you do. I bet I can find out. Wanta bet?" I lost him. *"Quieres apostar?"*

I still didn't have him. "No. I have nothing to wager."

"How about your life? *Tu vida?*"

His eyes told me he was catching on. "No. *Por favor,* mister."

"Where's Pedro?"

"No. I can no say. Pedro is very bad man. I die."

"Now or later. You choose, Paco."

The eyes were scared, lips trembled. Paco had a dilemma to solve.

Raleigh said, "Goddam, Sloan, this ain't no fuckin' Spanish class. Let's move on."

I crooked a finger at Paco. He stood his ground. I grabbed the wayward lock of hair and led him to the sink. "Know what that's for, Paco?"

"No." I think he did.

I didn't have enough Spanish to put it across. I pointed to his head. *"Cabeza. Ahogar. Comprendes?"*

He comprended. "No. Please, mister. No do this."

I nodded. "You give me Pedro or I'll drown your fucking ass right here in this nasty sink, Paco. Where's Pedro?" I laid my gat on the stove. Time to play.

I thought he was going to cry. I saved him the embarrassment. I shoved him in front of the sink, put a leg between his, grabbed his bound hands in my left, grimaced, and put my fingers in his well-oiled hair. I put Paco's head in the sink. "Count for me, Raleigh."

"One thousand one; one thousand two; one thousand three . . ." We went to one thousand thirty. Paco was ready for a little air.

He sucked in loudly, coughed a little. I couldn't see his face. *"Bastante?"*

"Sí."

"Donde está Pedro?"

He cursed me in Spanish. I guess. It wasn't friendly.

"Look, Paco, that was just thirty seconds, okay? *Treinta segundos.* Next one goes sixty. *Comprendes? Sesenta? Sesenta segundos?"*

He called me a pubic hair. Hurt my feelings. I put his head back in the sink. "Count me, Raleigh."

"You'll know when the motherfucker's had enough."

"Just count, Raleigh."

"One thousand ten; one thousand eleven . . ."

At forty, Paco started dancing. It was all I could do to keep his head down. Big bubbles started rising and I could hear him making noise in there.

Sixty. I jerked his head up. It sounded like an airliner powering up. He went into a coughing fit. I guess he tried to breathe a little water.

"Bastante?"

"No. Por favor, mister. Please, no. I cannot say Pedro."

"You've got to, Paco."

"No. I cannot."

"Ready for ninety? *Noventa segundos? Listo?"* I wasn't sure my Spanish was accurate. It didn't have to be. He understood.

Paco started hyperventilating in anticipation.

"Here we go, Paco. *Noventa.*" I put him in. "Count."

Raleigh was bored. He had lost his enthusiasm and wasn't counting.

"How am I supposed to know when we get to ninety, Raleigh?"

"I'm estimatin'."

Paco started dancing again. I pushed harder, bringing his feet off the floor. He kicked out at my legs, bubbles coming up like Lloyd Bridges was in there with him. I felt warmth on the leg I had between his. Paco had pissed on me. "Goddamnit. What you got, Raleigh?"

"Give him a few more."

"I don't really want to drown the fuck."

"So let him up."

I did. He scared me. He didn't move, didn't suck air, he just hung there limp as a wet biscuit.

From deep inside, it sounded like a train approaching. Slowly then faster. He lost the air in a gagging cough, fought for some more, got a grip, and went for broke. He huffed, puffed, and coughed for a few seconds until he was just breathing rapidly again.

"Ready for the two count, Paco? *Dos minutos?*"

The greasy head attempted to shake. "*No. Ya basta, por favor.* I will give Pedro."

"Hey, Raleigh, there's a break in the case."

We worked a few seconds on getting Paco back to earth, then a little longer to get an address in Metro West. I didn't think he was lying, but who could know.

"Raleigh."

"What?"

"Your turn. Think you can get your guy up and swimming?"

He did. Got a congruent story with less effort than I had used. With all due respect, one look at Paco and the guy on the floor was ready to chat. Raleigh still dunked his ass twice. No one counted.

It was time to roll. I said, "What do we do with these two kids?"

"We could kill 'em."

"Let's don't. Got any other ideas?" I did, but Raleigh had a better one.

He opened the bag, dumped a couple or three grams of doojee on the dinette table. He rifled around in the kitchen until he found a drink straw, cut it in half, threw it on the table.

Paco was first again. Raleigh cut him loose, put the AK to the back of his head, and said, "Snort."

Paco didn't get it. Raleigh showed him, a dry run, then pointed to the pile. Paco's eyes said he couldn't believe the turns life had taken lately. One minute, you're watching *Tres Veces Sofia*, next minute you're scuba diving in your kitchen sink. Then you're snorting heroin off the dining room table. Livin' *la vida loca*.

Raleigh made Paco vacuum up a half load or better, then got his compadre. Same deal. Raleigh and I talked while we waited on the smack to kick in, decided to put the brown bag back where it was. Raleigh did it, locked up, replaced the key.

When they started to nod off, we walked them out to the green '84 Chevy in the carport, loaded them up. They looked peaceful, snoring softly, off in Morphos.

I followed Raleigh to the Racetrack gas station across from Thirty-third Street and left them snoozing, pockets full of medium-grade heroin, waiting on the cops we'd called from a pay phone.

Raleigh and I laughed a little, thinking what the cops would say when the birds told them the story of their adventures. They'd be back on the street in eight to ten months. I was betting they'd go the fuck back to Puerto Rico. Raleigh concurred.

He also concurred with my idea that it had been a lousy evening and a midnight run on the house in Metro West would be way testy tonight. We'd hit them tomorrow morning, nice and early. Early to Raleigh was about ten.

I liked it. I had some ideas I'd need to set up. Decisions to make. What to lose; what to take. I dropped Raleigh at his hutch about one with a promise of another check.

Maybe Red Crider had more smarts than I had assigned him. He certainly had far more resourcefulness than I'd credited him with. I don't understand rednecks and it follows that I don't read them well. I'd flat-out missed the call.

His two-story red Dodge pickup sat somberly in the dark when I rolled in my driveway. My reaction divvied up a smile and a curse. Poor fuck. No doubt worried shitless. I hoped he wasn't looking for a fall guy, someone to punch around. I had over a half foot on him, nearly a head, close to that much in reach. I was still more than a little apprehensive. I'd misjudged him once. I didn't want to do it again.

I shut my engine down, half expecting him to be leaning over the car door when I opened it. He wasn't. He was nowhere to be seen. I hoped he hadn't kicked his way into my apartment. No on that, too. Everything was still intact.

I used my key on the door and hit the lights inside. No Red. I threw my trench coat on a chair, stuck my gun in the kitchen cabinet, and went back out.

Red was lying down in the seat of his truck. His face was slack and boyish in its pudgy jowlishness. I almost let him sleep, then decided I may as well get it over with. I didn't want to do it out of a dead sleep when he awoke at three or four.

I hit the window on the driver's side and he jumped, swiped a hand over his face, snoozed on. I hit it again. "Red."

His head jerked up, eyes squinting, face confused.

"Come on in, Red."

He sat up, rubbed the face some more, shook the sleep off.

I headed back in.

Behind me I could hear his door pop, hear him slide down to the concrete. "Hey!" too loud for this hour in this neighborhood. I turned to shush him as he rushed me. As I set up, I said, "Red, damn it, don't do this."

He came on, moving pretty good, going low like I'd expect from someone built like him. It was going to be a bullfight. And me without a cape.

"Red, think about it."

The train kept coming. He put a low growl to the effort. I let him get close enough so he thought he had me, arms coming out for the sweep. I stepped right, bent my waist to miss the sweeping left. His anticipated tackle left him pushing on air for balance. He went down face first, arms outstretched with less fanfare than I'd expected. There was a decent grunt.

He recouped quickly for having taken such a plunge, was on hands and knees coming up again.

"Red, goddamnit, knock it off."

"I'm gonna knock it off. Right after I kick your ass, mister."

The guy was having a bad day, but I didn't have to let him take it out on me. A guy like Red ever gets his hands on you, he puts you down and hurts you. You're on his level then.

I backpedaled about ten feet, giving him room for another good run. He took it.

This time I faked right early while his eyes were still opened, then stepped left two wide paces and put a foot in his right thigh. That leg fouled the left and he went down on his left side hard.

I circled around his feet while he couldn't see me, put another foot in his gut. He grabbed at it and almost got me. The kick came on him slow and he slumped down, frustrated and near tears.

He was off the concrete now, on the lawn. He grabbed two big handfuls of grass and clenched it in his fist, still facedown.

"Damn it, mister." His head went down and he cried like a baby.

I felt like shit. It wasn't my fault, but I still felt for him. The thing this simple man loved most had been taken. I didn't know how he felt. Everything I'd ever loved, I'd just pissed away. I know how that feels.

I sat down on the grass far enough away that he couldn't grab me. I put my voice low and gentle. "Red, I know where she is. You wanta help me get her back or you wanta roll around on the yard some?"

The blubbering stopped. He rolled on his right side so he could see me. A big fist swiped at the tears, streaking dirt across his cheeks. He looked like a little boy, all puffed and confounded.

"You know where she is?"

"Yes, sir."

"Where?"

"I'm not telling you tonight."

The Irish flashed in his face again. He sat up. "Then maybe we need to roll around on the yard some more."

"I hate to be the one to point this out, but so far you're the only one rolling around on the yard."

"I can change that."

"Won't do you any good. I still won't tell you. And you don't show me you know how to control yourself, I may change my mind about your going with me in the morning."

Red was back to normal. Slow thinking. He put the crystal blue eyes on me. "You know where she is?"

"Yeah."

"Both of 'em?"

"Yeah."

"You think they're aw right?"

"I hope so, Red. That's part of the deal."

"That hundred-and-fifty-thousand-dollar deal you was talkin' about?"

"Yeah."

"Mister, what the fuck is goin' on here?"

Goddamn, I was getting tired of telling this fucking story. I figured Red had suddenly become as vested as anyone this afternoon. "Come on in. I'll run it by you. But no questions and I tell it one time. Got that?"

"Yes, sir. Thanks, mister."

"And quit calling me mister. My name's Sloan. Not Mr. Sloan. Not mister. Just Sloan." I stood, brushed off the ass of my jeans, put a hand out, and jerked Red Crider to his feet. He followed me in like a puppy dog. A big, red puppy dog.

Red said he didn't drink coffee and I don't at night so I got to it. I told the story once more. What I figured he needed. I emphasized what bad-asses the Quesada posse was, hoping he was listening. "You still want in?"

"Why, hell, yeah."

"You got that Mossberg Home Defender in the truck?" The smile tugged at my mouth.

"Yes, sir."

"You think you'll be able to use it, need arises?" I was dead into his eyes.

"On the son bitches that takened Peggy Lee? You bet yore ass. Be glad to."

I shook a finger. "Don't be too damned froggy, Red. And for God's sake, don't you shoot me or this other guy who'll be with us."

"Who's he?"

"An ex-DUKE boy."

Red put a whistle through taut lips. "Them's some bad boys."

"Yeah. Mussolini's finest."

"Huh?"

186

"Never mind. Watch where you point that thing. The ladies will be in the house, too. Sheetrock won't stop that double-aught buck. Keep that in mind."

"Yes, sir. What do I do?"

"I have no earthly idea, Red. We'll figure that when we read the house." I stood and stretched. Another long day. "You're the guest, so why don't you take the couch. I'll make do on the bed." It was a joke wasted on slow Red. He thanked me.

21

Raleigh Lightstep's face when he saw Red Crider was priceless. I'd thought of a dozen of ways to do the introduction thing. In the end, I just walked in with Red in tow. No nothing. I did have a good grin going though.

"The fuck is that?" Raleigh looked like I'd brought George Wallace by for breakfast.

I put a puzzle on my face, then an "oh yeah," and said, "This is Red Crider. He's got a Mossberg Home Defender."

It was too early for nonsense in Raleigh's world. "Yeah?"

"Yeah. Red, this is Raleigh Lightstep. He's a Semper Fido, too."

"Hey. Pleased to meet you." Red put out a hand. Raleigh looked at it, back to Red, back to me. "The fuck is this?"

"Trust me, Red, Raleigh wakes up, he's a lot sharper. He gets on past the-fuck-is-this, the-fuck-is-that-stuff. He gets real nasty. Don't take it personally. It's just a defense mechanism. He's really a lovable guy."

Raleigh still hadn't joined up with reality. "Sloan, me and you, motherfucker." He pointed to the hall.

We went down it, went in the room with the safe. He closed the door.

"The fuck you bring that cracker peckerwood to my house for? Shit, I barely tolerate your white ass. I oughta slap shit outta you, Sloan. The fuck's a Mossberg Home Defender got to do with it either?"

"I don't know. He's an ex-marine and he seemed real proud of that and the hundred-dollar shotgun."

"Where you find that bastard?"

"The dump in Apopka. Keene Road landfill."

Raleigh shook his head. "It's early for this shit, dog. You gone have to tell me somethin' keep me from throwin' you and that cracker off the balcony."

I gave it up. It had been fun though. "His wife's the girl's sister. He was at the house when I got there last night. He was with the team that pulled Noriega outta Panama." I shrugged for him.

As I remember, my grandma could have pulled Noriega out of Panama, but it got Raleigh's attention. "For real?"

"He seems kinda rednecked, but he doesn't hit me as a liar."

"You think he can put out? In a tight spot, I mean?"

"Who knows. He can watch our backs though. Give him a shot, Raleigh. He's got game. I know that."

"How you know that?"

"I put him on his face twice last night, and he was coming up for more. The two of us might still be rolling around on my front yard if I hadn't told him he could come."

Raleigh paced some, thought some, cussed some. "What happens we ace these motherfuckers. He gone keep a secret?"

I shrugged. "Let's go ask him."

Red knew he had been the topic of discussion, his face said he did. He looked like a little boy again.

"Red, this may get nasty. Let me rephrase that. Me and Raleigh expect this to get nasty." I slowed down to Red speed.

190

"We're not cops. Not even close. We're just some citizens about to go shoot our way into a house full of junkies. Crazy fucking junkies. Who take hand tools to people who won't talk to them just right." I gave him some catch-up. "This isn't some video game. This is flesh and blood, assholes and elbows. We gotta, we're taking these dudes out. Clean and clear. Do the thing, grab the ladies, haul ass back to the house."

Red was doing okay. His face was growing up quickly. "I'm ready. Point me in the right direction. I ain't gonna let you down. Neither one of you." He was looking me and Raleigh in the eyes. Strong and steady.

"Good. One more thing. The part about not being cops. You get that or do I need to lay it out plainer?"

"You mean what goes on there stays there. We don't never bring it up again?"

"Good man, Red. No matter what. The cops ask you, you don't know me. You never saw Raleigh. You don't know shit. You get pinched, that's your ass. Don't make it me or Raleigh's ass." His eyes said he got it.

"Yes, sir."

"Then let's get going. It's a ride out there and I need to make a couple of stops. You follow me and Raleigh."

Raleigh opened the safe again, passed out the Kevlars, grabbed some playthings, and we booked.

First stop was a pawn shop. I bought a secondhand lawn mower and a beat-up gas can. Next stop dragged wild-eyed Jack out of bed. I gave him a few minutes to twist a joint, put him in with the equipment in Red's tall truck, and convoyed out to Metro West. I stashed Red and Jack at McDonald's. Raleigh and I went to locate Pedro's new *casa*. Not a problem.

It was one of those stucco jobs that will one day soon be so cracked and fissured as to represent an era of foolishness in construction. The concrete-skinned house with the rotting wood skeleton. The Orkin Man's recurring nightmare. A termite terminal.

The street was a cul-de-sac backed up on a retention pond. I pulled down a few streets until I located us across the pond, pretty much out of sight. We could see the east side of the house, the side the garage was on.

I ran my scheme by Raleigh, he shrugged, which I took to mean he didn't disagree. I asked him if he had anything better; he told me to make my call.

"Hallo."

"Pedro, *que pasa?*"

"Hey, asshole. You still alive."

"Sounds like it. You ready to let me make you rich?" He wasn't listening. He was telling his partners in crime the *gringo loco* was on the phone. They cheered. Sounded like two or three of them.

"You got my money, hey?"

"Soon. This afternoon about five. That work?"

"Yeah. I hope I can wait. I'm gettin' horny. Them skinny white girls lookin' okay. Know what I sayin'?"

"Come on, Pedro. They're pregnant."

"Yeah? So fucking what, hey? My dick fit in a pregnant girl. Maybe you hurry, I don't get so edgy, huh?"

"You got a good handle on the language."

"Yeah? Good Catholic school education. You calling to chat or what, asshole."

"Yeah. I get lonesome when I can't communicate with people. Fucking Paco, that bastard barely can carry on a conversation."

We stalled. Spanish being tossed around, too fast for me.

"Who is Paco?"

"Come on, man. You know Paco. He's one of the motherfuckers house-sitting for you down in Poinciana. Walnut Drive. You remember? Where you and Manny lived. When Manny was living."

More Spanish. A laugh. "You think I gone trade Paco and Enrique for the girls, you crazy, *hombre*."

"Trade? Heavens no. I'm just knocking the odds down. You know, in case you fuck up and give me a chance to bust cap on your ass. There's only two of us. How many left in your posse, Pedro?"

"Don't you worry, *pendejo*. We still got the odds on you. And hey, you try busting caps on me, you ladies gone bleed. You hear okay, don' you?"

"It's your call. We do the swap, maybe we can go *hombre a hombre*. You like to play, don't you?"

"Maybe we do that. First we do the money. How you find that house, hey?"

"Manny's rap sheet." I could almost hear him sigh relief. "Where you at now, Pedro. Maybe I could swing by and see you."

"Goddamn. You a funny man, asshole. No, you stay where you at. We deal when you get my money, okay?"

"Sure, Pedro. Listen, just for your info. You got any stuff at the house, you might want to get someone to swing by and pick it up."

Quiet, then, "Why that?"

"Before I took Paco and his buddy, what's his name? Enrique?"

"Yeah."

"Before I took them by the jail on Thirty-third, they got all flustered, couldn't find a key. We couldn't lock up. Hey, you know the neighborhood."

"Yeah. Fucking Puerto Ricans steal you blind, hey?"

"That's you talking, not me. Anyway, the house is wide-ass open. See you, Pedro. Listen for me about five or so. You got a place to trade?"

"Yeah."

"Where?"

"Why you need to know now? You want to set me up?"

"Love to. Be talking." I dropped the connect.

I looked at Raleigh and grinned. "How was that?"

He shrugged. "We'll see. They got to be thinkin' 'bout that bag of slow-down. Question is, how many of 'em it take to go get it."

"I'm hoping honor among thieves is bullshit. I'm betting on at least two going. Maybe all but one to stay with the girls."

"Don't try and predict the criminal mind, dog. Cain't be done by the layman. Trust me on that."

Ten minutes later, the garage door came up. A full-size van, a Dodge it looked like, backed out.

Raleigh put the field glasses up. "Well, I'll be goddammed."

"What?"

"It a family affair."

"How many."

"Three of 'em, it look like. The women, too." I got a rare Raleigh grin.

"Excellent. Let's go get Mutt and Jeff."

Seems there had been some spatting going on at the McDonald's on Hiawasee while Raleigh and I were away. Jack had fired up the reefer he'd rolled for his early-morning herbal enhancement. Red had grabbed it away and tossed it out the window. Jack had retrieved it and gone off behind the strip center next to Burgersville to sulk. And smoke.

I retrieved Jack, got a dollar's worth of gas and a quart of oil at the 7-Eleven. I put Raleigh in the truck, much to his embarrassment, with Jack; took Red with me.

Jack was to be dropped at the house. He was going to take his time about cutting the grass. Not a problem for Jack. Remembering what he was there for was a problem. Taking his time wasn't.

Raleigh was going to knock on the door, explain that the landlord sent them to do the yard. That's if anyone was home. We didn't think so. Raleigh would go up the street, do a cell to cell, let me know. Red and I would be on the street over behind the lovely green retention pond.

Ten minutes, my cell chirped. So far, so good. We could see Jack meandering around the backyard, following the lawn mower. I found two pairs of latex gloves in a pocket, handed one pair to Red. He looked at me funny. "In case we have to stick a finger in someone's ass." He looked at me even funnier. "Just put them on."

I grabbed the two Kevlar vests Raleigh had provided, and Red and I made our way around the pond to the side door of the garage. I tricked it with a credit card, hoping against hope I wasn't going to hear an alarm. I didn't.

I boosted Red up to the two-by-two access panel in the garage ceiling, tossed up his Mossberg. I tried the kitchen door. Unlocked.

It eased open on its own to quiet. A comforting sound. I threw the safety on my Smith and sent it in ahead of me. Nada.

I punched in Raleigh's number.

"Gotcha."

I didn't respond. I clipped it on my belt, connection open, and moved through the house. It wasn't bad. Decent furniture, fairly clean. Funky stuff like you find in a beach condo. My thoughts that it was a rental job were confirmed.

I played the whole joint. Nada still. Luck was holding.

The back bedroom had two windows. Plywood had been screwed over them. There were fast-food wrappers and refuse on the nightstands. The girls' cage.

I lifted my phone, said, "Got it, Raleigh. Northwest corner."

"You in there?"

"Yeah. Red, too."

"Watch that motherfucker don't shoot your ass with that piece of shit."

"I hope I don't see him until this is over."

"Yeah, well, I could do without never seein' his ass again."

"You want his truck, don't you?"

"Fuck you."

"See you in a bit."

"Yeah." He was gone.

I cruised around the house for a bit, being nosy. There were a couple of handguns in the master bedroom, a Llama 9 millimeter, and a cheap knockoff of a military .45. I relieved them of their firing pins and put them back the way I found them.

The fridge was a wasteland. Three Coronas, one Dos Equis, a two-liter Mountain Dew, two slices of leftover Dominos, a suspect pack of bologna, and a jar of Miracle Whip. No food in the cabinets. A couple of ounces of powder though. Coke or junk. Who cares.

There was a disappearing staircase in the hall. I grabbed the string and pulled it down with a lot of groaning and twanging of spring. "Hey, Red. How you doing?"

"Hotter'n hell."

"Don't pass out on me."

"I ain't gonna pass out. I could use a drink of water."

"Hang on." I got the Mountain Dew and tossed it into the dark. I could hear Red crab-walking over to it, then I could see him. He was pretty moist.

"When do I come down?"

"I'll yell for you. Hang on when the flash grenade goes off. I don't know what these fucking things do."

"They make a big bang. Stun hell outta whoever's in the room."

"See ya, Red." I closed his flap.

I wandered back in the bedroom fitted out for Crystal and

196

Peggy, wondered if they were enjoying the family time, how they were dealing with the loss of mom, granny, and dear step-daddy. Wondered why Red hadn't mentioned the fact that the rest of the family was in the county morgue. Maybe they weren't that close. That's what Doc Partain had said. Maybe he and Peggy didn't care.

The closet was empty except for the body armor I'd tossed in there. I moseyed out to the living room and flopped in an uncomfortable wingback chair. I could hear the lawn mower outside making slow rounds, getting closer to the house. Nearly finished in back.

The remote was on a side table of light wood. I punched power. Channel 62: Telemundo. Some blonde woman with dark roots and eyes the size of manhole covers was rapid firing at guests in chairs. The audience laughed. I didn't get it so I punched power again, got up, paced some more. Jack was on the south side of the house now, lawn mower droning to and fro.

The garage door made noise; the van pulled in the drive and stopped. A man got out of the driver's side and yelled at Jack. The van came on in the garage. I hustled back to the closet.

Inside, I pulled the door shut, flipped the safety on my piece, and dialed Raleigh.

"Uh huh. I seen 'em."

" 'Bye." I went quiet. So did the lawn mower.

I heard the kitchen door open, heard Spanish, heard a feminine voice say, "Don't push. We're goin'." A scuffle, then a soft pop.

There was movement outside the closet door, a male voice, heavy accent, said, "You be quiet. No talkin'. Don' fuck up. You got me?"

A feminine voice: "Yeah, we got it. God," the last sarcastic.

The male voice: "Hey, you watch you mouth. You need another slap?"

The female: "No."

"Then you shut the fuck up. Okay." It sounded like Pedro.

The door closed on quiet. Then whispering. The lawn mower started back up outside. They bought it.

The garage door made noise and the kitchen door opened and closed again. There was some Spanish, some laughing, more Spanish, more laughing. No doubt on Jack's tab. I was thinking, Laugh away, motherfuckers.

There was moving around in the house, the TV came up, the volume got punched way up. Somebody yelled, *"Baja el volumen."* The TV noise went back down. After that, there was quiet talk, less moving about. They had settled in.

I put a shaft of light between door and jamb. The women sat together on one of the two single beds. One blonde, one dark-haired. Other than that, they could have been twins. Peggy's eyes were red from crying. Crystal's face was red on the left side, I supposed from the slap. They sat in silence, Crystal's arm in a comfort gesture around her sister's shoulders.

As silently as I could, I eased the door open, dropped my brow to a warning, put a finger to my lips, and stepped out.

Crystal saw me first, nearly gasped. She quickly moved the hand from Peggy Lee's shoulder to her sister's mouth. Both looked at me. I could have been the Christ child, the looks I got.

I held up a vest, motioned with a finger. Nobody got it. I flapped a hand impatiently and Crystal came to me. I fitted her in a vest and whispered for her to put a blanket over her shoulders.

She couldn't stand it. She whispered back. "Who are you?"

"Your fairy godmother. Be quiet."

Her eyes went bewildered, her tiny mouth started to speak; I put a finger to her lips; pointed her to the bed.

I got Peggy over, fitted her, whispered, "Red's here, honey."

She gasped a little. I did the shush sign and pointed up. "Be a good girl. Do like your sister." She tried a smile; got tears. The lawn mower went off outside. Someone in the living room spoke to someone. More laughing.

The mower fired off again, coughed, died, fired up. It ran about as well as it had originally, which I was proud of for a piece of shit from a pawn shop, then it began to cough. I didn't have to look outside to know the yard would look like someone needed to call Red Adair. It would look like a Texas oil fire.

I had told Jack to shut the machine down after the *ticatos* got back, put all the oil in the fill port it would hold, tilt it sideways, and put some more in. My boy had done good. We'd wait for phase two. The mower died. Next move coming up.

The door bell rang and I could hear the guys cursing, someone gave it an *ay ay ay, ay, mucho humo*. Yeah, I bet much smoke. Get the door, fuckheads. Someone did.

I could hear Jack's voice. He'd be telling them he needed to call his boss. Tell him the mower fucked up. Someone yelled for Pedro. A toilet flushed somewhere, a door jerked open nearby, someone, I assumed Pedro, said, "Yeah?"

An explanation in Spanish. Pedro cursed, said, *"Un momento."*

The girls were staring at me like I was a secret escape hatch. Maybe I was. I mimed for them to pull the blankets around them and stepped back in the closet. I really wanted to stand there and put a tunnel through Pedro's head. I closed the closet door.

The bedroom door opened, Pedro stuck his head in, said, "You beetches keep quiet. I mean it. You don', you will be sorry." He closed the door.

When I could hear him talking to Jack at the front door, I came out, whispered, "Get up."

They did as told. I moved one of the beds away from the wall quietly. Again a whisper, "Get on the floor behind the bed." Again, they followed orders. I tossed both mattresses over them, pushed the bed back.

I leaned down and looked in their little fort. "Show time,

ladies. If I say run, you run like hell. Don't stop for anything, anyone. Get out of the house."

A blonde head and a dark head nodded.

Red's truck rolled in the drive as quietly as a July thunderstorm and died. I could hear Raleigh yelling. Playing pissed off wasn't a stretch for Raleigh. He always seemed pissed to me.

There was some laughing and some Spanish about the *gordo negro*, not a compliment in that language. A loud banging on the door. More laughing, movement. The door opened.

Raleigh was doing it up good and dark for them. "My boy say y'all fuck my mower up." Really yelling.

"You *loco*, motherfucker. Get away."

"Somebody gone pay fo' my fuckin' mower, Spanish."

"Hey, you watch you mouth."

"I don't care you got a gun. Somebody fixin' to pay me somethin'."

Yep, it was show time. Jack would be doing about ninety down the street on foot. He was a resourceful boy. He'd get home on his own.

I pulled the flash grenade from my belt, pulled the pin. I counted like Raleigh had said: one, two, three, quickly. I jerked the bedroom door open, heaved it at the living room, slammed the door shut.

Glass gave way everywhere in the house. Someone screamed, a man's scream, deep and creamy. The sound of caps being dropped came from the front of the house. One of the girls was coming out, blonde, Peggy. "Get back in there, goddamnit. Now!" She did. I hyper-breathed three fast ones, jerked the door open, put the Smith 9 millimeter up, and let it lead me out. I pulled the door shut after me.

A guy was coming out of the kitchen, saw me, raised a shotgun, and took away the doorjamb next to my head. I put two in him. He stumbled forward, hit the floor, and rolled, putting the shotgun back at me. I gave him two more. He stopped moving.

I moved down the hall, gat out, jumpy as a cat. One of them came around the corner of the living room and ran right into me. I went down on my ass. He got off a wild shot and jumped in the master bedroom on the left, slammed the door. The door splintered and I ass-walked into the bathroom. The guy was trying to hit me through the door.

I punched four in the door to back him up a little.

"Raleigh!"

"Yeah?"

"Just wanted to hear your voice." I dropped the clip on my piece and fed it a new one.

"Stay where you is. They one down there with you somewhere."

"Yeah. I got a fix on him."

"They one behind the couch. I popped him but he still kicking."

A shot came from the living room. "That you?"

"Hell no. It the fucker behind the couch. I cain't get at him." It sounded like Raleigh was still outside.

I went down on the floor and eased out into the hall. The couch was against the far wall from me. I said, "You ready. I'm gonna flush him."

"Go."

I put two about three inches off the floor under the couch. A big guy came up, couch going over. He had a revolver in each hand, one dropping cap at Raleigh, one in my general direction, not doing any good at me.

Raleigh's big .45 spoke once. The guy's head hit the wall so hard it crunched in the Sheetrock. He flopped forward on the overturned couch, both revolvers firing one last volley.

"Thanks, Sloan."

"That's what I'm good at. Flushing 'em out. There's still one in here. In the bedroom."

"Uh huh. That the bossman. I think he blinded. He turnt and the flash got him right in the face. I kicked him back in the door and he run smack into the wall 'fore he come your way."

"Yeah, well, he's not toothless. He's shooting at sound. Not doing real bad either."

"Where your peckerneck?"

"In the attic."

"Get him down here with that buckshot."

"Red!"

The attic stair slammed down and Red hit the carpet, went down, rolled once, came up sweating. He did a 180, made it a 360, saw me lying on the floor half in the bathroom, half in the hall. "You hit?"

"Nah. Just resting for a minute. I was you, I'd get my ass down. There's a guy in that room right there," I pointed with my piece, "shooting at anything he hears. Watch this." I got to my knees, grabbed a bottle of mouthwash off the vanity in the bathroom, went back down, throwing the bottle at the door. Three holes punched through it to go with the ones already there.

Red jumped back about three feet. "What you gonna do?"

"Hang on." I got to my feet, stepped in the tub, out of line with the door. "Put that Home Defender to work on the door-knob, Red."

He did. Second pop, the door slammed back. You could hear someone moving around in there. I came back to the hall.

"Hey, Pedro. End of the line, Holmes. You tapped, buddy?"

He went across the room like a flash, hit the wall, into the master bath.

Raleigh showed up behind Red. "Motherfucker probably deaf, too, Sloan. Shit, I damn near is."

"You must be. You're fucking yelling."

Raleigh put some mean muddy eyes on me. "Fuck you, Sloan."

Red looked around at Raleigh. I guess he didn't understand the intimacy of our relationship.

"Look here, we got to get the fuck outta here, dog." Raleigh had a finger in an ear, wobbling it around. "We done made a lot o' noise."

"Suggestions?"

We could hear banging from the other side of the walls, then something gave way, more banging.

It took me a second to click on it. "Oh fuck, the bastard's going through the wall."

Raleigh and Red didn't get it. They didn't have the lay of the house like I did.

"He's going in there with the girls."

Red hit the door like it was the beach in Panama. It went down, splintering what was left of the jamb. His timing was exquisite. Pedro stepped through and into two quick loads of double aught. Most of him went on the wall.

Next is kinda hazy. Someone started screaming for Red. Red threw the mattresses back, dropped the Mossberg, and had Peggy Lee up in his arms running.

I grabbed his gun, grabbed Crystal, pulled her to her feet, and pushed her at Raleigh. Raleigh got her high on an arm and went for the door at a long stride, long enough that Crystal was nearly running.

I started grabbing spent shells and jamming them in my jeans, trying to count. I knew I had dropped ten. Those I got. I got Red's four shotgun shells. I didn't know about Raleigh. Two, maybe three. Outside I was on the ground by the door on hands and knees.

Raleigh saw me, yelled, "I got 'em, dog. Let's roll."

I ran to Red's truck, threw the Mossberg in the back, said, "See you at Red's place in Apopka." I went around the house, skirted the scummy pond, fired up my car, and booked.

Two blocks up the street, when I stopped at a four-way, I realized I was shaking like St. Vitus. I was so bitched on adrenaline I was thinking I might never come down.

22

Some grass, some dirt, a Rottweiler puppy, an above-ground swimming pool, a dead '78 Camaro, a redwood picnic table, a six-pack of Budweiser on the table: Red Crider's backyard. Me, Raleigh, and Red in attendance; the sisters inside coming down, happy to be alive and well, and not much worse for the wear and tear.

Red was having a rough go at what had gone down. The guilt monster was gnawing on his ass. The more reality set in, the better grip the monster got.

"Well, I think we need to go to the police."

I looked at Raleigh, trying to hold my face blank. Raleigh's was, other than slightly raised eyebrows. "Why's that, Red?"

His face didn't know why. We'd see if his mouth did. "Hell, I don't know. Seems like what you do when something like this happens."

"You've got experience, then? With something like this?"

"Well, no. But . . . hell, I don't know." He made a mask with his hands, the golden hairs glistening like garnets where the sun made it down through the pine boughs.

Me and Raleigh traded looks again. Raleigh was getting nervous. I could see I-told-you-so all over him. I winked. "Let me run a few details by you. Help you out here. A guy pointed a sawed-off shotgun at me. Pulled the trigger. Lucky for me, he hadn't had a lot of practice. I dropped two caps on him, knocked him down. He pointed it at me again and I gave him two more. Sounds real close to self-defense.

"Another guy jumped up from behind a couch, points a big-ass revolver at Raleigh. Pulls the trigger. Raleigh's been around the block, moves out of harm's way. Hands the guy a nice soft forty-five slug. Still sounding like self-defense." I let it float out there. Let Red's geared-low gray cells have at it. I took a social sip from the carbonated beverage masquerading as beer in front of me. "Now, you." Effective pause. I put a double-handed, palms-down, thumbs-and-fingers-out wobbling-rocking thing on him. "You put two rounds of double aught on a guy for climbing through a wall."

Red took the hand mask off his face, dropped his jaw enough to show me his tongue and a double epiglottis. A dumb-ass expression of injustice.

"But my wife was in that room." Red was looking about as smart as I'd seen out of him. "And she'd been kidnapped. Don't that go for nothin'?"

I shrugged, posted a little frown over it. "A good lawyer might make it sound okay. Who knows what the twelve in the box might think. You may be right. The state prosecutors usually aren't as good as what twenty, thirty grand worth of lawyer will get you. It's your call, my man."

If he didn't give his head a break soon, steam was going to start puffing out of his ears. He put the face back in the hand mask. "I just don't know as I can live with this. Livin' scared it'll pop up sometime. Scared I'll wake up in the middle of the night with it."

"Oh, you'll do that for a while. Trust me. But it'll eventually start sleeping all night. Like a new baby. Give it time. Think about what could have happened to Peggy and Crystal if that motherfucker had gotten in there with them. Found them under those mattresses. Put his gun to one of their heads." I gave it a beat. "Pulled the trigger."

Red moaned behind the hands. "That's what I keep thinking. Me trying to work and raise Shawna. Worst of all, being here with no Peggy."

"How about doing five to seven at Starke while Peggy's here raising two kids. I think they pay you about seventy-five cents a day if you work while you're up there."

Another moan.

"Listen to me, Red. Look at me."

He put the hands away, the nearly transparent blues misty. He put them on me, tightened the jaw the way southern men do to fight the dogs of emotion.

"You don't have to go ask the cops if you did the right thing. You don't have to let a jury of your peers decide for you either. Nor let some slick-ass lawyer and a mean-spirited state prosecutor deal away your years like Old Maids." I leaned over, tapped him with a finger over his left breast. "Right there, Red. That's where you answer is. Right inside. Red Crider's heart. Did you do what you thought was best for you and your family?"

He nodded. "Yeah. Yeah I did. Wasn't no choice." He looked at me and Raleigh, weight coming off his shoulders. "Was it?"

Raleigh and I were mirroring head shakes. Raleigh said, "You coulda let him kill your wife. I don't see that as much option though."

I gave Red a good-old-boy slap on the arm with the back of a hand. "There you go, Red, my man. Raleigh might cuss you, ignore you, point out your faults. But he won't lie to you. And he was a cop for a long time. Let it go. Put it to sleep. It'll go away."

Red put a bunch of air in his chest, turned it loose, said,

"That's what I'm gonna do. Ain't no good gonna come totin' it around. Thanks, fellas." He pushed himself up from the table. "I'll go get Crystal for you." He looked at us like he was afraid he'd insulted us. "Y'all are welcome to stay as long as you want. I just figured you was ready to go."

"Yeah. Go get Crystal. And, Red." I put my flat stare in him. "This ever comes up, me and you and Raleigh were out fishing on the St. Johns this morning. Got it?"

"We catch anything?"

"Yeah. Two keepers. Threw the rest back."

I saw the first smile from Red Crider I'd ever seen. I hoped he'd keep them going. He made me nervous as hell.

When the storm door had hissed shut and clicked, I looked over at Raleigh. He was almost grinning. "Godam if you ain't one silver-tongue devil, dog. I ain't seen that much shit since the wall at the county waste treatment plant collapsed."

"What makes you think that was shit?" I just wanted to hear what he had to say.

Raleigh actually smiled, shook his head. "You got the boy thinkin' you all 'bout watchin' out for his ass."

"Well?"

"All I seen in there was your ass. And you coverin' it like a cat cover shit."

"Notice your own ass in there? Dog?" Raleigh put out a hand. I slapped it.

Raleigh Lightstep had shocked me when he accepted Red's offer for a ride home. A picture I'll always cherish. Big, dark Raleigh, sitting high and proud, up there with short, ruddy Red, Peggy Lee and baby between them. Raleigh's eyes focused like a kid's, working the shifter, putting muscle to task backing the tall Dodge out onto County Rose. Hammering it ahead of a plume of blue smoke, not much more noise than the Delta terminal at Orlando International. Red had let him drive.

23

Crystal and I hadn't gotten much of a chance to chat yet. Before I went to work on Red, I'd simply asked if she'd just go and listen to Pike's offer. Told her he was a nice guy and that being told what to do was over. Her choice. Listen; take it; leave it. She had nodded her agreement.

I could feel her eyes on me going up McCormick Road. Met her eyes when I stopped at the sign on Ocoee-Apopka. I couldn't tell if she wanted to fuck me or figure me. It didn't much matter. I knew what I had in mind and it didn't require pulling my pants off.

When she spoke, I found her voice more resonant and mature than I had predisposed from our whispery exchange at the Quesada hideaway in Metro West. She was baby faced, and I guess I was thinking her voice would match that. It was a nice voice with less cracker than I would have bet on.

"So why did you do this?" A hell of a place to start, but her choice.

"Money. Why'd you do it? Same?"

She shrugged in my peripheral. "I guess. You didn't know Manny, did you?" I guess that was an answer.

"Unfortunately, no."

"You're being a smart-ass, aren't you?"

"Yes."

"Are you all the time, or do you not like me?"

I grinned. "Crystal, honey, I don't have much opinion one way or the other about you. I don't understand what you and Manny were doing, fucking with someone's life like you did Ike Pike's. And I don't get titty dancing. It embarrasses me."

"Why does it embarrass *you*? You don't have to pull off your clothes."

"Because I have to share air in a world where people are desperate enough to get naked for money. Sell cooch for money, sell the same old thing for money. But more than that, I'm embarrassed to share air with motherfuckers low enough to put the money out there with no thought about the lack of whatever it is. Empathy; sympathy. Whatever it is that makes them take advantage of another human being. That make sense to you?"

"Not really. Sounds sorta old-fashioned to me. Why can't people do what they want to without having judgment passed on them?"

"Hey, you asked. I don't pass judgment on anyone. Not out loud anyway. Unless I'm asked; you asked. And maybe I am more old-fashioned than I'd care to admit. So what?"

She was smiling, looking prettier than the picture of her I'd been showing around. "I still don't get it. If it's my choice, what's the difference?"

"Okay, I'll give you some choices. You pick. Would you rather shake tit in a smelly, seedy strip joint, or be going to college to, say, learn a profitable profession?"

"I can't afford to go to college."

"I didn't hear myself ask if you could afford anything. Two choices. Pick one." I could sense her squirming around over there. I had trapped her and she was uncomfortable. "Let's say you could afford either."

"It doesn't take anything to dance."

"Oh, yeah? Maybe a little self-respect. You loaded with that?"

"You're making this hard."

"No, I'm not Crystal. The answer's easy. It's just hard to say. Go ahead. Pick."

"Go to school," came out quickly, somberly.

"Okay, we're getting somewhere. Next scenario, you know what a scenario is, right?"

"I'm ignorant; I'm not stupid. Okay?" She was getting testy. I was glad.

"What would you rather do? Shake tail at that same scuzzy, smelly tit joint, let's say, like the Sugar Shack on the Trail, getting down and dirty for creeps that take showers in cheap cologne, rubbing your naked ass with grubby fingers, leering like they could have the cooch for another five bucks and you'd be grateful for the opportunity." I looked over; Crystal had her head down. She might have been verging on tears. I hoped so. I pushed harder. "Same grubby fingers shoving dollar bills in a fancy garter, like a dollar actually bought something anymore. Pulling you against their rock-hard fantasies. Making you bend over so they can see the muff from a different angle. Slapping the cheeks of your ass like it's their God-given right." It was nasty. I was making myself ill.

Then the healing salve. "Or." I glanced at her for a second. Traffic was thickening so I couldn't give her a good stare.

"Or what?" She wanted to hear.

"Or would you prefer putting a nice steamy CD in a nice sound system sitting in the living room of a decent two-bedroom apartment you share with a guy who looks like . . . who do you want him to look like?"

211

She shrugged tiny shoulders. "The guy from Counting Crows."

"Okay. He looks like Adam what's-his-fuck from Counting Crows. Cleans his fingernails after work. Hits the showers once a day. Loves you like you're the last breath of fresh air in town.

"He's sitting back, fresh outta the shower, cold beer, in a big comfortable chair. Eyes soft and gentle. You're doing a slow strip for him. He's loving it. He's got enough control and respect, he let's you pump him up like an inner tube. Your song finishes, you come over and put a bare knee on each side of him. He puts the beer down, puts his arms around you, says you're the finest thing he's ever seen. Touches you down the back with just his fingertips. You stand up, take his hand, lead him to the big king-size bed you share every night. Roll like thunder; come like a train wreck." I gave it exactly one half beat. "Choose, Crystal."

Silence. She pulled her legs up, put her head on her knees, and began crying softly.

"Did I hear you choose?"

"You're a bastard," came out with a sob. "You're making fun of me. You know I'm trailer trash. I grew up in fucking Bithlo, man. People like me don't have lives like that. I'm trash. I'll always be trash. All I know is trash."

We had backtracked up the East-West to the Bee-line, me and my E-Pass jumping toll booths, blowing through them at seventy. "Baby doll, being trailer trash is not a life sentence. Not unless you choose it. It's a state of mind. It's a fucked-up start in life. But it is not a life sentence. You want it to be?"

Her head shook, still buried in the knees.

"Good. Because you're about to get to look behind door number three. That's the one that gets you outta where you think you're stuck.

"I'm gonna take you to meet someone who's your door number three. He's one of the finest, gentlest people you'll ever meet. One of the most sensitive, caring, compassionate people on God's green earth. Despite what you and Manny did to him, he'll treat you like royalty." She peeped at me, put the head back in its roost. "He'll give you enough money to take you far, far away from Crystal Johnston. All the way to Ms. Crystal Gail Johnston. Educate you, take care of you, watch over you, probably for the rest of his life. This is the golden ring, Crystal. Don't blow it."

The head lifted, turned toward me. She didn't get it. Too much of people wanting everything for next to nothing. "What does that make me. His whore? Why's that better'n what I'm doing?"

I laughed at the windshield, shook my head. "No. This guy wants one thing from you. Well, maybe two. He wants his baby that you're growing in your tummy there. And he wants you to be happy. See, Ike Pike's gay as they get."

Crystal's eyes squinted up. What I'd said wouldn't spark and catch fire. It was out of bounds in respect to her expectations. Then she got it. A laugh started as a girlish giggle, exploded into a roaring, tear-flowing laugh, shaking her light frame, bouncing her shoulders. The lifetime of rip-rap she'd been buried under had been lifted. I think for the first time in the kid's life, she was looking forward to tomorrow. Looking forward to being a free person, someone who could make her own choices, free and clear. The laughter slowly subsided. I wouldn't say died; I'd say it went back inside her. I hoped it would stay with her for a long time.

She yawned and leaned her head against my shoulder, snuggled in, both hands on my arm. "What's your name? Duncan?"

"Yeah."

"What do your friends call you?"

"I don't have any friends."

She poked me in the ribs. "What do people you know call you?"

"Sloan."

"Sloan, will you be my friend. I mean forever?"

"I'm trying, Crystal. Goddamn, I'm trying."

24

Three raps on the door that said 670 got Reggie and a grin. "Hey, Duncan. Come in." He wanted to know who the little elf with me was, but he didn't ask. He just went and got Ike and Steve Glass.

Pike showed, smile ready. Glass nearly smiled. They both took the hand I shoved out. Glass and I were making progress, be it slow and rickety.

"How's Don?"

The smile grew. "Conscious. They may have to strap him down to keep him in bed."

"Yeah. He thinks he's on duty twenty-four, seven."

Pike rolled his eyes. "Yes, I guess he has been for a long time. We're discussing that."

"You get another body servant sent down?"

That got me some blush. "No. Steve and I have decided to make some changes. We're moving to New York. I'd like to get the number from your friend there. See if he will possibly introduce us around." His curiosity was gnawing him. I let him get gnawed.

"This Steve's idea?"

Glass grinned. "Sort of a mutual decision. There's not been much for us in St. Paul for a long time." He put an arm around Pike's waist. "Even less now that . . ."

"Yeah. I know what you mean. When you guys moving?"

Pike lost it. "Damn it, Duncan."

I put on a face for them like I'd had an Alzheimer's episode, then, "Oh, yeah." I turned and put a hand out for Crystal. She took it. I brought her forward, presented her. "Ike Pike, Steve Glass, meet Ms. Crystal Johnston. Mother of you guys' baby. Ms. Crystal, fathers to be, Isaac and Steve."

Steve Glass handled it well. He stepped over, gave her a hug that looked genuine. "Love your hair that way."

Crystal went a little pink, eyes down. "Thank you."

Ike Pike stood, hand clenched against his stomach, his mouth kept jumping at the corners. The tears on his left cheek had a slight lead, maybe a head, over the ones on the right cheek, both heading for the finish line at his chin. His eyes would go from Crystal's eyes to her slightly meloned belly, then back up, back down. The mouth finally decide to smile and stay that way. The back of his hands made a quick trip to his face, pushing away tears. "I'm so pleased to meet you, Crystal."

Crystal pinked a little again, eyes shy but happy. "Thank you, Mr. Pike."

Pike moved forward, bringing Steve Glass with him, said, "There are no misters here, Crystal. Just Ike and Steve. Daddy and Papa." The three of them embraced.

I turned and headed for the door. I'm not big on emotional scenes, wouldn't be seen crying in public for money. Well, maybe for money, but never for free.

I grabbed the knob and opened the door. Pike said, "Duncan, thanks. Thanks for everything. I don't know what I . . ."

I flapped a hand at him. "I'll send you a bill. See if you still feel that way."

Crystal broke out of the clench, ran over to me, wrapped me in twiggy arms, head in my chest, tears fucking up my shirt. "Sloan, thanks. I'll stay in touch." She leaned back, looked up. "Is that okay?"

My hands were vagrants, they didn't have anyplace to be. I patted her head with one, rubbed her back with the other. "Sure, baby doll. I'm counting on it." I wasn't, but it sounded like what I was supposed to say. Like I said, I'm not good with scenes like this.

I broke the clench and went through the door. I started for the elevator, passed 666, home of my favorite hooker. I stopped, turned, had a fist in the air to knock. I caught it about six inches from the door, said fuck it. I got on the elevator and went back down to street level.

After all, street level is where I belong.